NEW YORK, NEW YORK

NEW YORK, NEW YORK

WHERE THE HUDSON FLOWS

A Film Story in a Script Form

RANJAN MUNSHI

PARTRIDGE
A Penguin Random House Company

To order additional copies of this book, contact
Partridge India
000 800 10062 62
orders.india@partridgepublishing.com

www.partridgepublishing.com/india

CATEGORY – STORY, DRAMA, FILM SCRIPT

Based On a story Kedargadh written by Ranjan Munshi

Story Line:

Life itself is a stranger with whom we walk along but never know where? Can life be governed? Or life governs us; we may not get the answer. Life is not a destination but unknown journey.

Life steers trough many lanes; narrow-wide, known-unknown, ancient-modern. Or many times through nostalgic when we steer and ride perhaps we may be lead to the unknown place where everything is new.

To whom we meet, or pass by is not in our hand; may be our destiny leads us somewhere and we begin our new journey.

When Kumar landed at New York after the tragedy of 9/11, these questions were rolling in his head. He was a stranger coming to New York for the first time. He was confused and perplexed.

By the time he settles down and be clear about his mission coming to New York some strange incidents happened. He met Anita the New York Times reporter.

Both never knew when they met and their first encounter took place that their story would end soon. It happened.

Anita was a Cancer patient and in her final stage; she was admitted to ICU, her conditions fast deteriorating and end may come anytime. Kumar was besides her; she was breathing fast, difficult to talk as she was struggling to say something.

Kumar took her into his arms as she desperately trying to be in his embrace; silence prevailed; chilling moments thrilled both, she uttered her last words," I Love you", Do you?' and closed her eyes forever.

Tears rolling down Kumar felt he will go mad, he in slow trembling voice said, "yes".

A smile appeared on the departed soul.

AUTHOR'S NOTE:

The story has reference to the Hudson River estates.

It would be proper to write on the beautiful Hudson River as it is a backdrop of the main story. History of the river makes it more romantic and scenic to enjoy the story or a movie.

"Since Henry Hudson sailed the Half Moon up the Hudson River in 1609, great men and women have been drawn to the Hudson Valley's bounty and beauty. Politicians, artists, businessmen and socialites built fabulous estates up and down the river's banks, each adding their own unique contributions to the area's collective history.

As members of the American aristocracy, these modern settlers were able to hire the best architects, landscape artists, and decorators to build their palaces.

Their legacy includes some of the finest examples of several historic architecture, landscaping, and interiors, from the early Federal period to the numerous revival styles of the late 19th and early 20th century. It is our great fortune that many of these estates have been meticulously restored and lovingly maintained to recreate each home's historical and cultural significance, as well as personal character. The estates along the river recreate a history not only of the Hudson Valley, but of the

United States, contained in a many layered contextual experience.

There is a rich history wrapped around the men and women who settled along the Hudson River. Statesmen and politicians called the Valley home, including Franklin D. Roosevelt, whose estate at Hyde Park was both his refuge and his final resting place. Several estates in the Mid-Hudson region are connected with various branches of the Livingston family, whose members included war heroes, political figures, and one of the five authors of the Declaration of Independence (who, incidentally, swore in George Washington as the first president of the United States).

The Mills and Vanderbilt families were at the center of New York society life at the turn of the last century, their estates redolent with the opulence of the American Renaissance. The Hudson Valley's lush landscapes drew artists to its beauty, inspiring the Hudson River School of Painting. Some of the finest known examples of this artistic movement are on display in Olana, home of Frederick Church. The estates in the Valley are as varied as the people who built them. From Clermont's Federal austerity to Lyndhurst's Gothic castle, popular trends in American living over the course of our history are represented here, in their finest state. Unparalleled architecture in a diversity of styles, exquisite landscaping and gardening, and superior collections of artwork, furnishings, historical archives, china and silver, textiles and other treasures are maintained in their period condition. The residences are replete with familial details and personal possessions that convey a sense of home, a memory of having been lived in, and a deeper understanding for the people who lived there. At times, it feels as though the family has just stepped out for a walk, giving the visitor a chance to poke around the house before they return.

Several organizations oversee the estates of the Hudson Valley, providing the attention to detail and dedication to preservation that allows these wonderful estates to flourish in modern times. Historic Hudson Valley, a nonprofit organization started by John D. Rockefeller, Jr., oversees the Sleepy Hollow region estates of Sunnyside, Philipsburg Manor, Kykuit, and Van Cortlandt Manor, as well as the Montgomery Place estate in Annandale-On-Hudson.

BEGINNING

A prince from Kedargadh, an old Riyasat and former Princely State in Rajasthan comes to New York City. His arrival coincides with 9/11 tragedy; almost a week later, when flights were resumed. It was an evening; flight was late and he took time to come out of the airport.

He came with two distinct missions, one to find out where about of his grandfather Kedarnath who had an office at the World Tower Two. This head quarter of billionaire businessman Kedarnath was ruined and gutted into the fire and now what remains is debris and rising black smoke covering the 'City'.

The second mission was to find out his American mother who gave birth to him and then reported lost.

The same time at the New York Times office, the night staff taking over from day shift reporters and assistant editors; a young lady still in teens took over and relaxed a bit; a phone rang, it was from Immigration office at the airport; the lady picked up and heard what was reported; left for Editor's chamber and after some time returned; picked up woolens; shoulder's bag and swiftly left. She picked up a cab and moved away.

THE SCENE OPENS….

Camera

This is JFK International Airport.

It is evening and the arrival lounge.

Announcement:

'THE AIRINDIA FLIGHT FROM INDIA HAS ARRIVED.'

(Camera pans the exit and catches the hurry burry of the busiest airport. the multi color dressed folks anxious to welcome their guests are looking here and there. They are talking among themselves with inquisitive faces. A typical airport environment in view that is full of noise and unevenly gathered people, a crowd.)

CUT TO

(Camera, A transfer or jump within the scene)

EXT: (EXTERNAL/ OUTDOOR) THE AIRPORT LANDING GROUND, A DAY

THE AIR INDIA AIRCRAFT SLOWLY COMES TO A HOLT.

CUT TO

EXT: THE OVER SKY, A DARK DAY

(The thick clouds gather, hide the setting sun, it suddenly starts drizzling.)

CUT TO

EXT: THE AIR CRAFT AIR INDIA, A DAY

Camera zooms to the opened door of the aircraft; the 22 years old prince, tall, six and above, very handsome, broad shouldered, wavy hair, well groomed, smiling comes out and turns to air hostesses at the entrance with folded hands and murmurs 'Namaste' and then gradually starts descending the steps.

CUT TO

FADE IN:

EXT: OUTSIDE THE AIRPORT, ON ROAD, A RAINY, LATE EVENING

The Mercedes carrying prince Kumar is making its way through the heavy evening traffic. Kumar looks out, perplexed as the buildings pass by and people walking on road.

(The expression of awe and wonder appears on his face. He is visiting the American City for the first time.)

Camera zooms on him and covers him.

He turns his head inside and wants to talk.

He turns back and looks out.

The darkness is descending; head lights of moving cars are on, heavy traffic makes cars move slowly. As if the 'Fall' is to arrive soon leaves begin to change colors of the trees adding some cheers to the City which seems to be perplexed. Evening breeze is pleasant but the events that happened a week ago had snatched away the mood of the City. 9/11 looms large on the 'City', the hidden silence prevails that is evident on the faces of his co passengers in the car.

Kumar is on a secret visit. He remembers India and the glory of Kedargadh.

Flashback (In a quick sequence)

Kedargadh is a beautiful town surrounded by mountains and gardens. A majestic Palace stands imposing over a town that had proud history. It is close to the desert of Rajasthan, fortunately a small river flowing through the town provides greenery and distant mountains of Arvalli range give it a heavenly look. Kedarnath the ruler was known as benevolent and progressive ruler and is loved by the people. He modernized the town with textile mills and industries; gave jobs to many and made it a prosperous town. He brought best faculty to teach at Kedar University. Similarly he invited highly qualified doctors to run the hospitals with all the amenities.

After his wife passed away he left for USA and settled there. His business acumen helped him to expand his business to global level and attracted world famous leaders of corporate world; politicians; scientists; artists and leading Americans in his circle. He started 'The Manhattan Club' which became famous and a Foundation for Humanitarian aids.

He held large and expensive properties in and around New York including many Manors and Mansions on the Hudson River all along upward; he remained a ruler though lost his Kedargadh but enjoyed palatial buildings of past with romantic backgrounds.

He was staying close to but opposite to the World Trade Center facing the Central Park. He had his office at World Trade Center and saw from his apartment the actual attack on both the buildings gutting into the flames and tumbling down. The latest news of him was not available when Kumar left for New York.

He is suspected to be missing after 9/11 tragedy.

Kumar saw all this as a flash while travelling with strangers in his car.

Kumar is the grandson of Kedarnath family. He loved his grandfather and always remained in his contact.

The news of 9/11 tragedy made Kumar's visit to new York immediate. He was at Bombay when he received a call from Marry, Kedarnath confidential secretary and reported him what had happened.

FADE IN:

EXT: BOMBAY, AIRPORT'S RESTAURANT, ALMOST A MID NIGHT (PEVIOUS NIGHT)

Kumar, Paul and Lisa are sitting in a restaurant. Paul and Lisa are Kumar's friends who have come to give him a send off at Bombay Airport; Paul is world renowned photographer; Lisa is a leading fashion designer.

PAUL

Kumar your visit to New York is a secret visit. You will never forget that you are going on a very important mission.

LISA

New York is a typical American city; it is friendly and beautiful metropolitan City. The River Hudson flowing all along the New York State. It is also mysterious and challenging, when you are going for the first time it means you need to hide your real identity or show as if nothing has happened.

PAUL (lighting a cigarette)

Kumar it is coincidental that you are visiting after a week of 9/11. New York has not settled after the shock. I came back only day before yesterday. It is horrible.

I had no time left at New York after returning from Florida as flights were irregular and schedules changed periodically. I failed to inquire about your Grandpa. It made me worried.

KUMAR

Paul you are right. I am leaving for New York without informing any one at Kedargadh; you know that Tantric Swami and my mother would follow me and try to even kill me. I love my grandfather. (He becomes emotional)

LISA (putting her hand on Kumar's shoulder)

Kumar we know everything. We are sure you are going to save your Palace and your grandfather.

KUMAR

Paul and Lisa, I found a diary that revealed another secret that my real mother was American who gave me birth in New York hospital and died in mysterious conditions. After my father died in plane crash no one knew about that. He mentioned this in his diary which is now I possess. All these years I knew that Radhika is my mother. God should not place anyone in such a tragic situation. Professor Roy is in America and now in New York and that is a great solace and comfort to me

PAUL

I think Kumar better you call yourself by some American name and don't say who you are and what for you are there. Better u call yourself Kane; (laugh, I mean Citizen Kane. (The mood of three becomes Light.)

KUMAR

Paul I never say anything that is not a fact. But you are right I should be cautious and on my guard.

I accept your suggestion to be known as a Kane.

PAUL

(Kumar is lost in deep thoughts.)

It's time for departure.

PAUL

Take care.

(He smokes and puffs out and the smoke fills the room.)

Kumar waves to Paul and Lisa.

(The United Airlines flight now left Bombay it is now crossing the Sea turning for onward journey.)

CUT TO

INT: (INTERNAL/ INSIDE) IN THE CAR, LATE RAINY EVENING

The Kumar is looking outside, his eyes are wet, few raindrops falls on him, and suddenly he becomes alert and remembers that he cannot be emotional. He turned his face inside the car.

He poses himself to be funny to hide his emotions. His mission to America must remain a secret.

KUMAR (LOUDLY)

I am Kane. (He laughs loudly.)

KUMAR (CONT'D)

I hope you know the famous film 'Citizen Kane'.

I was born here. (Again he laughs.)

KANE (KUMAR)

We have a Manor near Riverdale on the Hudson River.

(The lady sitting besides is amused to hear the prince, who is not arrogant, childlike and not that sophisticated. The curious gaze of the lady makes him conscious.)

(He becomes conscious and starts speaking slowly and looks nervous; but suddenly he feels that he is the prince;

he need not reveal his nervousness; he shows deliberately that he is confident and starts talking normally with American accent.)

MS. JUDY (She is Kane's care taker during his stay at New York.)

Oh. It is nice to hear that you are America born.

(The woman is middle aged, wears the specs and looks more conscious while talking.)

KANE

Yes but really I am an Indian Prince.

MS. JUDY

I am here to look after your stay in New York and as your care taker will be always at your command.

(The driver in the front is amused at the manners of the Prince.)

He turns back and gives a smile to the Prince. Kane responds with a nod.

CUT TO

EXT: ON ROAD (Almost night)

The rains start raining heavily. It is now dark and the headlights of the other automobiles are on. The wipers of the car wipe the water. The wipers movements are synchronized with Kane's thoughts.

(When I reach and see the devastation; fear that I may not see my grandfather, if I do not meet him then…?)

The moving wipers removed water, Kane stopped looking at wipers and came back to his senses. Mercedes was lost in moving cars and the cavalcade in the front

FADE IN:

The New York Times reporter came down and got into a cab; she murmured to the cab driver and they are on their way. Anita, the reporter chuckled in her cheeks for getting this assignment. She had just joined 'The Times' was looking for a thrilling story. The Immigration had said to her that a Prince has arrived from India.

Anita from her childhood had heard about Palaces and Princes, read some fascinating and romantic novels and she had dreamt meeting one Prince in her life. Her wish may be fulfilled; she thought and smiled; looked out and find normalcy returning to wounded New York. Her going to Hotel and inquiring failed to find that no Prince has arrived.

FADE IN:

EXT: THE CENTRAL PARK. NEXT DAY, DAWN

The grass is wet, the trees are green. Few men are cleaning the fallen leaves and other garbage. Birds are chirping in the bush. Few regulars appear to enter and start walking.

CUT TO

EXT: THE CENTRAL PARK EARLY MORNING

In one corner, a man is sitting with only half pant and nothing on the body in a yogic posture.

(He breathes through one nostril and breathes out from the other, the loud breathing sound stops the morning regulars in the park, and they look at him. Somebody remarks 'SWAMY')

CAMERA ZOOMS IN ON KANE

Kane is lost in the yogic exercise. His face is sometimes tense, some time relaxed and smiling; some time, his eyes brows are curved sharply. A close up continues marking changes on his face.

CAMERA MOVES BACK. THE FRAME IS LARGER.

A dog moves close to him, wags his tail and sits down. The changes on his face and the reaction on the dog continue. He stops waging and suddenly stars waging again.

He moves closer to Kane.

CAMERA MOVES BACK FURTHER, COVERS THE LARGE CANVAS AND ZOOMS OUT.

The thin crowd has started collecting near Kane. The youngsters' group also joins claps and starts whistling.

Kane opens his eyes in anger and the dog starts barking. The whistling continues and the crowd becomes thicker.

More persons join the crowd.

CUT TO

FADE IN:

EXT: THE CENTRAL PARK, MORNING

The sun shines. The clouds are dispersing. The birds are flying and hovering around in circle.

CUT TO

FADE IN:

EXT: THE PARK, LATTER, MORNING

Kane is suddenly gets up and try to find his shirt; he takes out the shirt from his shoulder bag and puts on in the presence of all. Every one rejoice and Kane yawns and says loudly 'Namaste'. Everyone in the crowd shouts 'Namaste'.

He laughs. Starts whistling; takes out a flute from his bag and starts playing.

(Kane's behavior is to create a different image and try to hide is real identity. He deliberately behaves to be typical Indian following rituals.)

FADE OUT

FADE IN:

EXT: OUTSIDE THE PARK, FACING THE FIFTH AVENUE, THE MORNING

Kane walks to his parked Mercedes and opens the door. He is about to enter when reporters and a crew of camera operators appear; they request him to give his interview. He nods but finds that he is not properly dressed.

KANE

Thank you. I am not properly dressed. Better, we meet at my hotel Hilton where I stay. I invite you all for a lunch.

(Kane laughs.)

REPORTER

No Sir, You are too generous and interesting too.

KANE

OK. We meet here.

Kane jumps to the hood of his car. He sits on the hood with folded legs and the hands; in between he waves to the passersby.

KANE (CONTD)

Ask me, what do you want to know about me?

A LADY REPORTER

Sir, May we know your name? How do you find the New York?

A reporter in jeans and white T-shirt comes forward and starts the conversation.

KANE

Call me Kane, the Prince. I love New York though this is my first visit. I was born here 22 years before. My mother was an American lady, daughter of a famous Jefferson family; very aristocratic and rich. My late father Avantinath was an ex ruler of Kedargadh, a state in India before the independence. OK.

A LADY REPORTER

Sir, Are you a multi millionaire?

(He laughs.)

KANE

No madam, I am a billionaire.

REPORTER

Sir, how long are you going to stay here? Is there any special purpose that brings you here?

KANE

I am going to stay for some time. I am America born. You people know that I have a huge palace at Kedargadh? It is marvelous, wonder of architectural beauty. Yes, I have a special purpose to visit this City.

A LADY REPORTER

Sir, please tell me more about the palace?

KANE

The Palace is more than one hundred years old; built in the beginning of this century.

REPORTER

How many rooms your palaces have?

KANE

I have only one palace. It has three large halls, twenty balconies, eight huge terraces, and three-storey building. Totally, One hundred and sixteen rooms, sprawling garden of three hundred acres.

A LADY REPORTER

Sir, have you seen your entire palace at least once?

(A young beautiful girl reporter of eighteen chuckles, smiles with mischievous eyes.)

Every one laughs. Kane joins them.

He now gets down from the hood and joins the group.

KANE

I know my palace in details. I can draw the map without being there.

He moves close to that girl and with a twinkle in his eyes politely ass the young lady.

KANE (CONT'D)

Would you like to be my guest at the Palace?

Kane moves closer to her and looks straight into her eyes; she stares in his eyes and then moves away. Kane marks her pale face behind her hastily made make up.

CAMERA ZOOMS IN ON THE BOTH, FREEZE.

Both smile to each other.

FDAE OUT

FADE IN:

INT: INSIDE THE CAR, A DAY

The cell phone rings, the tall, the American African driver with large face and long jaws picks up a cell phone from his shirt's pocket; he switches off the car radio that is on when the cell phone rings.

ANDREW

Yes, Andrew calling. Yes Ms. Judy, Sir is busy talking to few reporters; yes, I will tell him.

He switches off his cell phone; opens the door and gets out, turns and looks for the Prince; he finds the Prince engaged in close conversation with the young woman reporter. He moves further, takes turn from the front of the car and makes way through the thin crowd of the reporters.

He politely tells the Prince.

ANDREW (CONT'D)

Sir, Ms. Judy called back; she has requested to return to Hotel room; it will be time for your breakfast.

Andrew turns and starts walking back.

CUT TO

EXT: MERCEDES CAR, THE MORNING

KANE PUTS HIS HAND OVER HER SHOULDER AND BECOMES SERIOUS.

KANE

May I give you a lift and drop you at your place? Where do you work? How do I call you?

THE YOUNG LADY REPORTER

'ANITA'

I will certainly enjoy a ride with the Prince charming. I am working as a journalist with The New York Times.

CAMERA

They both turn to get in; Kane helps her to get in first. He closes the door. He moves to the other reporters and say good-bye and thanks. Then he moves on the other side of the car and enters as Andrew has already opened the door. The car moves

CUT TO

INT: KANE'S CAR, THE MORNING

CAMERA ZOOMS ON THE BACK SEAT

ANITA

You are very polite and considerate. I will never forget this moment when I am riding with the Prince in a Mercedes.

KANE

Anita, if I am not very snobbish, may I be fortunate enough to know more about you? When I looked into your eyes, I felt inside that there is some strange message in your eyes. I may be wrong.

He shrugged his shoulder while talking.

ANITA

You are right. I am diagnosed as a cancer patient.

(She tries to stop the tears rolling down. Andrew looks back and looks at the prince as if warning not to take much interest in any stranger.)

KANE

No; no please don't say this. You are so young and promising; you are very beautiful. God is great; He loves every one of us and cares.

ANITA

I shouldn't have told you all these in a short acquaintance; I am sorry. I forgot that you are a Prince; I am also sorry that we made jokes on you while interviewing; no one was so serious, but you were honest. That is great.

KANE

No, Anita I always wants to say what I believe; or follow my rituals; that are with me from my childhood; any country or its manners do not make any difference to me. Please forgive me for being boring and eloquent. Anita, could we be friends?

ANITA

A Prince and a reporter! How nice? May I ask you for your exclusive interview today; preferably, at your manor on the Hudson River? I have never seen a manor.

KANE

How do you know that I have a Manor on Hudson?

ANITA

Being a reporter, I collected some information and now I knew few things about you.

KANE

I will love to. Andrew will pick you up from your office in the evening.

DISSOLVE

THE SCENE DISSOLVES SHOWING THE CAR MOVING AHEAD WITH SPEED ON FIFTH AVENUE AND GETS LOST.

FADE IN:

INT: HOTEL HILTON'S MAGNIFICENT ROOM, A DAY

(The wall clock in the entrance corridor shows 9 O'Clock. It strikes nine as Kumar enters the room; he is greeted by Ms. Judy and another Indian, about 60-70 years OLD, in suit)

MS. JUDY

(While walking)

Sir, you are late; Professor Roy has been waiting for you since 8 O'Clock.

(Professor Roy belongs to British era; if you look at him you compare him with late Bernard Shaw. He is pipe smoker enjoys to smoke and gets lost in thoughts. He is a closest friend of Kedarnath, his confidant, guide, friend and philosopher in one.

Prof. Roy as he is known belongs to Shanti ni Ketan at Bengal associated with late Poet Laureate Rabindranath Tagore; he spent his childhood there, studied under Tagore's influence and then became a professor of Literature and Philosophy. His versatile mind always engaged him in many fold activities. He also played a significant role in educating three generations of Kedarnath, his son Avantinath and Kumar. He has investigative mind and approach; his vision and perspective are difficult to understand and follow. He is a visionary speaker and poet.)

PROF. ROY

Ms. Judy,

Kumar, better I call him Kane, he is not in hurry. I know him since his childhood when he came to Kedargadh when he was only four years old, mischievous more like hid grandfather. Kedarnath too loved him and they had several horse rides around Kedargadh when Kedar trained him in governance, religion and business. They used to continue their discussion after returning home and argue; I joined them too.

Today where is Kedar? My mind cannot get rid of this thought.

Kane is a different person; first he will like to take bath; then he will do pooja at the temple that has been set up near his study, and after that, he will sit for a breakfast.

Sorry for my long lecture Ms Judy, We Indians are talkative tribe.

(Prof. Roy wears one armless glass on his right eye. He has a habit of pampering his beard.)

(He is suddenly lost in some other world.)

CUT TO

FADE IN:

INT: THE BATH ROOM, A DAY

Kane enters in hurry, starts taking out clothes, first shirt, then pant; only knickers remain; his muscular body is all shining; he pampers his muscles, with palm measures both hands' muscles and smiles to him in the mirror; he starts shaving, singing an Indian film song very loudly. He enjoys singing.

CUT TO

MS. JUDY (SHOUTING FROM OUTSIDE)

Sir, get ready soon.

INT: THE BATH ROOM DAY

The shave is over, he opens the shower. Kane enjoys the shower, he recites auspicious Sanskrit slokas that are recited at the time of bath in orthodox Indian family; he closes the shower, picks up the bucket full of water and pours over him.

CAMERA ZOOMS ON KANE AND FREEZES. KANE'S PROFILE WITH DRIPPING WATER

FROM HIS HEAD AND NOSE BECOMES CLEAR
AND DISTINCT.

DISSOLVE

FADE IN:

INT: THE MAIN ROOM AT HOTEL HILTON,
THE MORNING

Prof. Roy is walking to and fro; then moves to the large
open French window and looks down. He is lost to view
the City from the above.

Camera pans outside from top of the suite and catches
vivid hundred and eighty degrees view of sprawling
'City'.

(The traffic and heavy rush down on the road is visible.
Prof. Roy smokes his pipe raises his head and looks at
the horizon. From the top floor the New York City is
visible, the panoramic view brings smile on his face, and
he puffs more and throws out smoke from his pipe. He
suddenly notices the smoke slowly rises from rubbles at
some distance; the two towers and hip of debris; from
the distant view the ruins reminds him of Kedar's office;
he withdraws back and closes the large window, returns
to his chair and slums down. He turns and murmurs)

PROF. ROY (TO HIMSELF)

Really, really the New York is enchanting; the most glorious and prosperous City in the world. But where is Kedar? Who knows? Billionaire's Empire has vanished.

CUT TO

INT: MIDLLE OF THE ROOM, A DAY

(Kane enters the Pooja room in his yellow silk dhoti, nothing to cover the upper part, open shoulders, sandal wood's 'tilak' on his forehead. Two Pundits, short, round faced with bulging bellies, thread on their shoulders hanging from their right shoulders in cross to the left of their bellies too enter behind Kane, they are reciting mantras for pooja.

Kane rushes inside the pooja room.

CUT TO

FADE IN:

INT: POOJA ROOM, A DAY

CAMERA ZOOMS IN ON THE LARGE IDOL OF LORD KRISHNA PLAYING FLUTE; BEHIND THE IDOL HANGS THE PAINTING WHERE LORD KRISHNA IS SEEN IN THE MIDDLE OF GOPIES

(WOMEN); PLAYING FLUTE IN YELLOW DHOTI WITH COSTLY ORNAMENTS.

CAMERA ZOOMS OUT SLOWLY AND THE FRAME EXPANDS, COVERING KANE AND HIS PUNDITS PERFORMING POOJA BY GARLANDING THE IDOL AND THEN THE LIGHTING THE LAMPS. THE GOLDEN ROUND PLATE WITH LAMPS IS PICKED UP BY KANE; THE CONCH IS BLOWN, THE CYMBALS ARE PLAYED AND THE BELLS RING PULLED BY THE STRINGS BY THE TWO PUNDITS. PROF. ROY; MS. JUDY COVERS HER EARS; ANDREW JOINS AND ENJOYS; THE ENTIRE ENVIRONMENT IS SURCHARGED WITH LOUD SINGING AND THE SOUND OF BELLS.

DISSOLVE

RIVERDALE

Riverdale's winding, tree-lined streets and stately single-family homes may make you think you're not even in New York City anymore. This tony, suburban enclave has been welcoming refugees from Manhattan's bustle and summer heat for decades.

On parts of winding Palisade Avenue on a recent morning, birds trilled, the air smelled of honeysuckle, and thick tree branches nearly formed a tunnel along the street. The appeal goes beyond the area's borders. Hugging a ridge, North Riverdale takes in views of the Hudson River and, on the opposite bank, the Palisades cliffs of New Jersey. "It's magnificent," said Margaret Segreti, a nearly 50-year resident. "Every season is beautiful."

70 leafy acres occupy the site of the 1850s former estate of the Shakespearean actor Edwin Forrest, including his neo-Gothic castle, was not alone in seeing the opportunity in huge tracts of land.

It is presumed that Kedar preferred to buy this estate and convert into retreat as well as his private office.

FADE IN:

EXT: MANOR ON HUDSON RIVER, NIGHT

CAMERA IN SLOW MOTION COVERS…..

IT IS DRIZZLING.

THE INSIDE LIGHTS ARE REFLECTED IN THE POOL WATER.

THE LIGHT BREEZE SWINGS THE TREES AND THEIR LEAVES.

Camera Freeze for few seconds,

FROM THE MANOR UPSTAIRS THE SWEET RHYTHM OF PIANO IS HEARD OUTSIDE,

CAMERA IS ACTIVE

CAMERA PANS THE MANOR AND THE GARDEN, SLOWLY ZOOMS IN ON THE POOL AND ZOOMS IN CLOSE ON THE REFLECTION OF LIGHT IN THE WATER AND FREEZE.

(The sound of the piano and the falling drops of the drizzling rain create a unique atmosphere.)

FADE IN:

INT: MANOR GUEST ROOM NIGHT

Kane strolls in the large verandah.

(He has put on his Indian dress. He is in a very serious mood. He sits back in the rocking chair and slowly rocks.)

CAMERA ZOOMS IN ON HIS FACE.

He closes his eyes.)

FLASH BACK

He is a cute and sweet child of four. He is playing in the garden. Suddenly some persons come rushing and drag him away. He screams Mother 'Mother'... These screams echo and rebound; every wall rebounds with these screams, 'Mother.... 'Mother.

He still hears those screams. Shut his ears and weeps.

He suddenly rises from his chair and moves to the table

He opens the drawer of the table and pulls out a photograph of his grandfather Kedarnath. He places the photograph on the table and with folded hands pray.

Behind on the large wall hangs a big panel showing a gigantic Kedargadh Palace.

KANE

I am your Kumar. Where are you? Where is my mother? I don't know anything. You left India and I was Left behind.

The tragedy of the World Towers has not left any trace and any remains of our empire you build from there. Where are You How do I find out?

He moves out back to the verandah, the wide open horizon with twinkling stars speak to him.

He listens.

The Hudson flows here, never stops; only winter freezes it. You young prince be aware that many centuries came and vanished but the 'Time' never stops; these stars always shine. These celestial planets and astral sky know the destiny of each soul. The world is deaf and the 'Sound of Eternity' is lost in the worthless noise of no importance.

He fears it is the voice of an Angel.

"Never look back and move ahead, there is a promise."

(He hears that the car has entered. He wipes his tears)

CUT TO

EXT: MANOR PORCH, NIGHT

Andrew opens the door and Anita alights. Anita looks around. The drizzle continues. She enjoys getting wet. Andrew shows her the way to the entrance.

CUT TO

FADE IN:

INT: STAIRCASE, MANOR, THE NIGHT

Kane is climbing down the staircase; he is half on the staircase, looks down.

CUT TO

Anita is climbing up the staircase. She looks up. A sweet smile is on her lips.

CUT TO

They both meet on the halfway of the staircase. Kane escorts her and they climb the staircase.

ANITA

Kane it is marvelous. Thanks for the courtesy shown to me.

KANE

It is my pleasure. I am honored by your visit.

Both laugh. They stop on the last step of the staircase before entering on the floor. Anita turns to Kane and looks at him. Kane holds Anita in his hands and then picks up her chin and becomes serious. A smile appears on her face.

FADE OUT

FADE IN:

INT: A GUEST ROOM, MANOR, THE NIGHT.

THE HUGE CHANDELIAR IS ALL ILLUMINED. CAMERA PANS THE TOP OF THE CARVED CANOPY. THEN THE CAMERA ZOOMS IN ON ANITA AND KANE. IT ZOOMS IN ON THE BOTH OF THEM STANDING NEAR THE KEDARGADH PALACE GIANT PANEL ON THE WALL.

Anita lights a cigarette, smiles. Kane is disturbed.

ANITA

Kane I really want to relax and talk. Leave all formalities and sit. Tell me why have you come to New York?

Kane doesn't reply. He takes his sit and avoids facing Anita.

ANITA (CONT'D)

Are you well? Kane you have become serious. What is the matter?

KANE

Anita I hope you wouldn't mind if I say something.

ANITA

Go ahead.

KANE

Why are you smoking?

ANITA

Don't be silly. I have been smoking since I went to college, may be even before.

She relaxes; she smokes and throws the smoke in a circle. Kane observes. He is annoyed.

ANITA (CONT'D)

You don't like any one smoking in your front? If that is so, I will stop it.

Kane gets up and strolls.

ANITA (CONT'D)

Well, I stop it.

(She extinguishes the cigarette. She gets up and moves to Kane. Kane is serious and avoids Anita.)

KANE (After some moments)

Forgive me Anita being indifferent and bit annoyed. Forget. Let us start talking.

ANITA (CONT'D)

Have I hurt you? Then I am sorry.

KANE

No. I was bit disturbed. For a moment I couldn't accept the whole situation. There are reasons for that. In India, ladies usually don't smoke and I was really worried about you.

ANITA (BIT ANGRY)

Worried about me? Oh. No. I am a professional person. I meet number of persons, interview them and move around a lot. I am a journalist.

KANE

Anita that is my weakness, I immediately establish more personal relationship and in your case I am more concerned.

ANITA

Concerned about me for what?

KANE

You know why.

ANITA

Thanks. Do we come to business?

KANE

Of course, ask me what do you want to know about me?

Both smile and look at each other.

KANE (CONT'D)

You asked me why I have come to New York. Listen. My story is absolutely personal. I request that you may not write what I want to keep secret, if you promise, we may proceed further.

ANITA

We journalist have ethics and we do understand the importance of the matter revealed to us. Kane, I am from a very reputed paper, no yellow journalism. Please trust me.

KANE

Anita, it is a tragedy of my life that has brought me to New York. I want to find out where is my grandfather whose where about are not known to me after the attack on World Trade Tower Two on 9/11. Our billionaire business head quarter was located on 11th floor and when the plane struck the Tower my grandfather was there. No staff is alive. In India my step mother was in fact interested to destroy him. She has been overpowered by a Tantric Swami who rules our entire estate and wealth at Kedargadh.

Kane becomes serious and is lost in thoughts.

ANITA

Kane you are afraid that you lost your grandfather but I lost my brother who was heading a fire fighter team. He was the only son of my mother. Even now The New York City is shedding tears, there is a gloom pervading all over.

KANE

Anita; as I told you I was here and my mother was American; I found from the secret diary of my father.

I need to find my mother's relatives. We don't know anything with our grandfather gone, I am in dark.

ANITA

Kane do you remember you asked me could we be friends? I said yes. I will help you to locate your grandfather and your mother.

KANE

Anita how can I involve you and get you loaded with more worries.

(Anita moves closer and stands very close to Kane and looks in his eyes. Kane is serious. Kane looks to Anita and unexpectedly picks up her hand and press between his two palms.)

FADE OUT

FADE IN:

EXT: OUTSIDE HOTEL HILTON, EVENING

Security is alert; cars arrive; aristocrat people get out of their cars and moves in through the porch; the cars are driven further; others follow.

CUT TO

FADE IN:

INT: A LARGE HALL, WELL DECORATED AND LIGHTED WITH CHANDELIERS.

The guest arrives and occupies the allotted seats, guided by the staff. Anita arrives with her friends and takes the seat in the front.

The Mayor Dr. Ionesco arrives. He is given the rousing welcome.

The procession of young girls and women in colorful Indian saris and costumes with copper pots over their head follows; Kane walks behind in tweed suits but with a royal turban over his head. The Shenai players accompany the procession. (Shenai, Indian Instrument similar to the clarinet)

Kane moves forward and shakes hand with the Mayor and few other celebrities in the front row.

An anchor requests Mr. Mayor and Kane to proceed to the rostrum.

(The anchor is an American young lady; clad in sari and flowers wrapped over her hair at the back; she appears to be uncomfortable and conscious at her silk sari that slips from her shoulder and she is seen in her blouse; she has put on big kumkum (Bindi) on her forehead.)

Mr. Mayor and Kane move together assisted by the staff; they walk toward to the steps, climb up and settle down on the dais; the audience is attentive and quiet.

THE ANCHOR

I invite your kind attention. Certain rituals will follow that proceeds before any auspicious function.

Persons in the front look to their left; two pundits who were at the morning pooja also appear; they come before the stage and stand with folded hands. To the surprise of all they forcefully breaks two coconuts and sprinkles coconut water on the guests in the front rows; the guests are dismayed and shocked and some get up from their seats; there is a heavy murmur all around. Some at the back rows clap.

The anchor announces.

ANCHOR

This is an auspicious ritual; the sprinkling of the coconut water purifies the total environment. The Lord Ganesh's blessings invoke that the ceremony will pass through successfully. I request Mr. Mayor Dr. Ionesco to proceed with the function.

Mr. Mayor gets up; Kane also gets up; they shake the hands; Kane takes out his turban and places on the table. (There is laughter in the audience.)

MR. MAYOR

Our honored guest the Prince Kane; ladies and gentlemen.

Today is a significant day for our City. Our country is multicolored and multiracial and respect all traditions and culture. We witnessed a grand ritual before our eyes.

(He laughs, Kane joins).

There is applause.

Kane gets up and bows down to accept the applause. He sits back. Mayor continues.

MR. MAYOR

Mr. Kane is the Prince of a by gone Indian State Kedargadh; his father and grandfather merged the State with the Indian Union after India got the independence. However, the royal family played a significant part in the development of our City; donated millions of US dollars, and created charities that benefit the citizens of this great historical City.

Our City has seen the worst ever event and we have lost many of our brothers. In that reference the charities helps and that is a great humanitarian act. This is the first visit of the prince; he was born here twenty two years before and has privilege that his Mother was

American and in a way he is an American citizen. (Again, there is applause)

Kane again gets up and bows down. The applause is louder with the laughter.

MR. MAYOR (CONT'D)

The City has decided to honor the Prince Kane as he visits this City for the first time and it will be my pleasure to release his first book entitled 'KEDARGADH - The Magic of Majestic Dynasty.' The book is a fascinating account of the glorious years of the rulers of Kedarnath, Kane's Grandfather and his Father Avantinath, who turned the small town into a prosperous tourist center and buzzing industrial town. I release the book with pleasure I thank the organizers for inviting me to do the job and I am sure the book will be very popular. Thank you.

He releases the book.

(Thundering applause)

THE ANCHOR

Now I request the Prince Kane to address.

KANE

MR. MAYOR, Ladies and Gentlemen

I never imagined that I will be in NEW YORK; my birthplace. (Applause) I am very happy to be here. This evening is going to be memorable. Friends, let me tell you that New York is the friendliest CITY. I find friends everywhere.

(He looks at Anita in the front row who smiles and clap)

KANE (CONTD)

I rejoice meeting them.

Coming to my book, it is the saga of my grandfather Kedarnath at Kedargadh. The palace there is the architectural wonder; my town is the small city in Rajasthan close to desert. However, In terms of wealth, we are billionaires; but we are very religious family and follow the rituals that look funny. However, let me tell you the secret.

All these rituals are in the Indian scriptures; they have deeper significance.

We do not have secret societies but open rituals that benefit all. I am an ardent follower of all the rituals. You will find the details in my book.

Like Citizen Kane, I am proud to be the in this City and I promise that our charities will be always there for the people. I share the grief that the City is experiencing at the present moment.

Thank you.

THERE IS A STANDING OVATION AS HE SITS BACK HE GETS UP TO JOIN ALL AND HE LAUGHS.

CAMERA ZOOMS IN TO CATCH HIS CLOSE UP.

FADE OUT

FADE IN:

INT: HOTEL HILTON SITTING ROOM, EARLY MORNING

(Prof. Roy walks and opens the windows and the soft morning light fills the room. It is breezy and cool. Roy puts his glass and picks up the newspaper. The front page of New York Times carries the photograph of laughing Kane's close up with the headline.)

'The Prince Who Is Not a Thief'

(Roy is amused for a moment.)

Prof. Roy folds the paper and with terrible pain on his face removes his single rim spec. He looks gloomy and worried. He moves closer to open window. He looks at the open morning sky and radiant colors spread over the horizon.

FLASHBACK

OVER TO KEDARGADH

The Sun spreads its warm sunrays over the Palace. Kedarnath returns from the morning ride. Prof. Roy is sipping the tea in the garden. Kedarnath joins him. He is tall and well built Rajput ruler, he smiles to Roy and pulls his chair and joins to have his morning tea. It was a routine that every morning he will go for a ride in different directions of his town and come back. It was a time to discuss with Roy important matters of family or business.

Kedar

Roy I am thinking to leave Kedargadh and settle at New York to look after our business that is expanding enormously beyond my imagination. My wife left me and I feel alone. Avantinath my only son has plunged into active politics and has no inclination or time.

Roy time has come that the legacy of Kedargadh will gradually fadeout. The Glory of this enchanting Palace will be lost. The long shadows will remain.

Those were the years, Roy, when Kedargadh was compared to the best run Riyasat. Britishers preferred to maintain the dignity of Kedargadh. The modern education, hospitals, art gallery, sports; theater all came here because of them.

Gandhiji was the moving spirit. We respected and followed him; we supported his movement. Anne's Gandhian Ashram was a forefront humanitarian place to serve the poor and handicapped; sick and needy. We were the only tiny State that accepted different situations wholeheartedly. We believed in harmony and peace.

We survived and flourished. We modernized.

Kumar, when he was brought from America was placed under Anne's care; Radhika took over as his foster mother.

Roy you joined our family, brought a new spirit from Shantiniketan; you planted in this soil the concept of beauty, refinement, cultural synthesis; encouraged new generation with vision and philosophy.

You became a modern Guru.

Kedargadh owes many things to you.

Time has changed."

Roy listened to Kedar and remained silent.

Kedar's decision was correct but then at whose care administration of Kedargadh be given?

Kedar as if understood Roy's agony said," Roy, you will be the caretaker and administrator of this old Riyasat."

ROY CAME TO HIS SENSES AND RETURNED TO HILTON HOTEL SUITE WHERE BEFORE MOMENTS HE FOLDED THE NEWS PAPER AND SAT DOWN.

CUT TO

INT: KANE'S BEDROOM, LATTER DAY

(Kane with the minimum clothes is sleeping with his face down and his back visible. The bed is scrambled)

CUT TO

INT: THE SAME ROOM DIFFERENT ANGLE, A DAY

KANE'S SIDE FACE; HIS WAVY HAIRS ALL UNORGANIZED; SLOWLY KANE OPENS HIS EYES AND STAIRS ….

CUT TO

INT: THE SAME ROOM OPPOSITE SIDE, A DAY

CAMERA ZOOMS IN ON THE PHOTOGRAPH ON THE WALL. THE NUDE BEAUTIFUL YOUNG LADY WITH ALL WINNING SMILE LOOKS STRAIGHT TO KANE.

CUT TO

INT: THE SAME ROOM, MOMENTS LATTER, A DAY

CAMERA THEN ZOOMS IN ON KANE

Kane jumps from the bed and covers himself with bed sheet; he starts reciting mantras and he is trembling. He shouts.

KANE

Who, on earth; placed this photograph?

Andrew rush in, looks at his master's situation and runs; Ms. Judy enters and screams and runs and bangs with Roy who also enters at the same time. Both fell down. Roy's specs flew into one corner and he struggled to get hold of it; he cannot see anything without the specs on. The Judy fell flat on the ground trying to take care of her as her gown was torn and her thighs were more or less exposed. She screamed and ran.

The shocked Kane accidentally throw out the bed sheet; he is almost naked; Roy closes his eyes and shouts:

ROY

Kane put on your clothes.

(Kane is standing; almost to weep; the smiling woman in the photograph looks on Kane without cloths in the background.

The camera movements during the scene need to be adjusted to bring out the humor that arises from the situation.)

CUT TO

INT: SITTING ROOM OF KANE IN THE HILTON HOTEL, A DAY

Camera covers the full portrait of Kane. (Kane is meticulously dressed and ready to leave,)

He murmurs slowly, "How long will he go on playing funny? Anita has suddenly come into his life. He never felt to be attached to any young lady in his life. What is in Anita? Her Looks! Her slim and beautiful Body! Her smiling and caring eyes! Or her fear and shock in her deep eyes! Her paleness and her diseases make him more inclined as sympathy?

He takes both of his hands up and holds his head in total confusion.

A thrill pass through his limbs, he shivers; he is perspiring. He wipes it with his scented handkerchief.

'Or, is he in love with Anita?'

"NO". He shouts; 'it is too early to judge'?

"Leave her alone? Do not proceed further."

'But, Anita? If she loves him, yes she is then?

A cell phone rings.

KANE

Hello!

Who? Oh. Anita, how are you, what? Are you speaking from the hospital? What happened? Please do not cry, listen... Now please listen, Oh. Do not cry. I am coming; now, now do not worry. Everything will be fine. O.K

Kane sits on the sofa; Roy comes near; Ms. Judy joins.

KANE

Anita, that reporter who met me and traveled with me from the Central Park tells she has a cancer and she is very uncomfortable. Call Andrew and tell him to take the car out and wait. I will have to go.

ROY

Kane you never told me about this. Who is Anita? Why are you so upset?

KANE

Prof. Roy Anita is a very intelligent young reporter from NY Times; she is only eighteen and so young and sweet; but she told me she is suffering from the cancer; I was shocked. Yesterday she met me after the function; she was well and suddenly she is in the hospital.

ROY

Kane some time you behave foolishly. You know that New York is a notorious City and many people have become victims of the cheats. Once they know that you are Prince and a billionaire, wealthy, they will try to tangle you in some fraud and that will be a disaster. I warn you.

KANE

Prof. Roy you always use your mind and never listen to your heart. Not all the people are like that. Anita is different.

ROY

Let me ask you; are you in love with this girl?

KANE

I am not sure but I have deep and real feelings for her. I have to go.

He gets up.

FADE OUT

FADE IN:

INT: LOBBY OF HOTEL HILTON, A DAY

People are coming in, People are going out. Elevator stops. KANE comes out. He is escorted; accepts Namaste from some people.

FADE IN:

EXT: HOTEL HILTON PORCH, A DAY

Kane walks to his car. Andrew opens the door. Kane gets in. Andrew closes the door. Takes his seat and drives.

CUT TO

INT: INSIDE THE CAR, A DAY

ANDREW

Sir, where are we going?

KANE

Andrew, Anita is in the hospital; she is in the Columbia University Medical Center, New York Presbyterian Hospital; I will like you to be driving fast; it appears that she is in the critical condition.

ANDREW

Is she in critical condition?

KANE

She is suffering from cancer.

ANDREW

God bless her. Sir, Cancer is dangerous.

KANE

I know, Andrew. She phoned me. She was crying.

ANDREW

She must be in real trouble; poor girl.

KANE

Andrew, Is it true that we have to help somebody when in serious trouble?

ANDREW TAKES THE TURN. THEY ARE PASSING THROUGH WASHINGTON BRIDGE.

KANE (CONTD)

Andrew, we are strangers, I met her only two days back; somehow I feel for her.

ANDREW

Sir, naturally, she is a very nice girl, very intelligent.

KANE

Do you know her?

THEY CROSS THE BRIDGE AND TURN TO RIVERDALE PARK.

ANDREW

Yes Sir. I knew her from her childhood. We were neighbors.

KANE

Andrew, tell me more about her. I am anxious.

ANDREW

She was very thin and delicate from the time I saw her; she would remain in her house and never saw her playing.

KANE

Why?

THE CAR TURNS AND ENTER THE CAMPUS AND THEN TO THE NEWLY BUILT MILKEIN BUILDING.

ANDREW

Sir, we have arrived; yes, she lost her father in the war and her mother was serving with a low salary in the Day Care. They were poor, but she was brilliant in her studies; I know that.

KANE

Do you know that she lost her brother in the blast at WTO? Andrew, you be with me. Park the car; I am waiting.

Kane gets down; Andrew drives to the parking lot. Kane looks at the magnificent South facade of the building and slowly loiters around and wait for Andrew to return.

Kane sees the magnificent Hudson River flowing; Kane is all praise at the marvel of the modern architecture. He moves to the South Facade of the new building. A panoramic view of Hudson River makes Kane speaks to him.

NEW YORK, NEW YORK, WHERE THE HUDSON FLOWS!

CUT TO

INT: INSIDE THE HOSPITAL, A DAY

Kane and Andrew walk fast and meet a lady doctor coming from the other side,

KANE

Good morning, doctor, we are looking for the cancer patient ward.

Doctor stops, gives smile.

LADY DOCTOR

Good morning, are you the Prince?

KANE

Yes doctor, but how do you know?

DOCTOR

If I am not wrong, the whole of the City knows you. Your photographs in media have made you a celebrity.

Kane Laughs loudly; Andrew looks at him and Kane becomes conscious that he is in the hospital.

DOCTOR (CONT'D)

Are you looking for any specific patient?

KANE

Yes, I am looking for Anita, a New York Times reporter.

DOCTOR

Does she know you? I am just coming from the conference where we discussed her case.

KANE

Yes. I met her two days back at the Central Park; where she was there with the other reporters. She asked me a funny question and I went close to her. She looked very pale and her eyes were deep with anguish, which I could read very easily. I offered her a lift and we traveled together, where she revealed that she was a cancer patient. She phoned me some time back at my hotel and asked me to come here. She was crying, so I rushed.

DOCTOR

Sorry to say but she is in critical stage and her cancer has advanced. She needs immediate surgery but she finds excuses.

THEY START WALKING TOWARDS THE WARD.

CUT TO

INT: ESCALATOR CLIMBING UP, A DAY

(While in the escalator, doctor turns to Kane.)

DOCTOR

May I know your good name?

KANE

My name is Kane; please tell me does Anita know about her condition?

DOCTOR

No. Fortunately not yet; however, Mr. Kane unfortunately she does not have anyone nearby. We tried to contact her mother, but she is hospitalized and they said they would inform her when her condition improves.

What a tragedy of life. If I may request you Kane then, please let Anita does not know anything about her condition.

KANE

Oh my God; I never imagined when I landed in New York; that, I will be facing such a delicate situation. Doctor, please tell me what can I do to keep her happy; I do not think there is any other alternative. I will pay for her operation. But she should not know.

DOCTOR

In our conference, it was suggested as one of the alternative that she should be helped to forget her condition and more care should be taken of her, and if possible to take her to a vacation, preferably among the Nature. Kane, I am also is confused. As doctors we rarely come across such situation. But she would need operation sooner or latter.

(They arrived on the floor and start walking.)

CUT TO

INT: A HOSPITAL ROOM, A DAY

(Anita is relaxing with her friend.)

Kane and Andrew enter.

CAMERA ZOOMS IN ON ANITA'S FACE.

PALE; TEARS DRIED ON HER FACE; SHE HAS TAKEN OUT HER SPECS, SHE LOOKS GLOOMY.

CAMERA MOVES BACK AND COVERS AT MID SHOT THE LARGER FRAME.

KANE

Hi. Anita.

ANITA

(While putting the glasses on her eyes)

Kane, I was waiting for you. I am so sorry I made you rush. What else I could do? You were the first person I thought of as soon as I reached the hospital.

KANE

How Nice? You thought about me. A friend in need is a friend indeed. (He laughs)

Every one joins.

ANITA

Kane, meet Ms. Audrey Kennedy, Miss America. She was here visiting her relative and we saw each other; she came to me. She is my school friend.

KANE

Good morning. Your friend seems to be worried.

Doctor says that she is better and nothing to worry. I met the doctor on my way.

(Audrey is very beautiful. She has a fine figure. She is dressed in jeans and shirt. She is quite tall, lean and very attractive.)

AUDREY (SMILING)

Good Morning Mr. Kane, Anita was just talking about you.

KANE

Anita, doctor told me that you need rest and perhaps a vacation; you are over worked these days that has made you sick. So, relaxed and have some change and you will be better. Anita, you are very lucky; doctor has found an excuse for you to go on leave and proceed to your dream vacation, a beautiful destination. (He Laughs)

AUDREY

Anita is lucky; look, I have been craving for a vacation, but that is simply not possible. (She also laughs)

(Cheers come to Anita. She smiles and calls Kane and Audrey close to her. They move; they sit close to Anita; Audrey on her left and Kane on her right.)

FADE OUT

FADE IN:

INT: MANOR, LATE EVENING SAME DAY

Kane is rocking in his chair. (Anita's face appears before him. Anita looks in his eyes.)

KANE (AS IF TALKING TO ANITA)

Anita your tearful face haunts me. Something deeper in my heart stirs me; I have never in my life had such feelings. I want you to live. You know that we are friends. When I think about me, my grief and agony is nothing. All these years I have been lonely without any warmth. I kept away from my Palace and my friends Paul and Lisa looked after me. Anita I am nobody, nobody loves me. Nobody is now to ask me how am I? I laugh at me that I am a billionaire Prince. A poor Prince; he doesn't want anything. No woman ever gave me love.

I don't trust women. I don't know why? I may be wrong. When we met Anita I felt that someone has entered my life. But then you too will leave me. (He sobs)

He gets up from the rocking chair.

He turns, surprised to see Anita who has been discharged from the hospital and came to his manor. She is standing in one corner and smiling. Anita has brought the bunch of roses. She gave those roses to Kane. Kane moves forward and takes roses and along with that Anita in his arms. Anita places her head on his broad chest. They remain quiet for some time.

Late evening sun has come out from the dispersing clouds. The rays are gradually filling the room through the open verandah. The horizon brightens up with many hues.

FADE OUT

FADE IN:

INT: AUDREY'S PENT HOUSE ON MANHATTAN, A DAY

Audrey lights a cigarette and waits for Kane to come. (Audrey is most modern and sophisticated lady; she is fashionable and wears costly jewelry. She is around twenty, a beautiful model selected for the Miss America title. Her life style is different from simple Anita. Audrey is studying for the Law. Her house is decorated with latest style furniture and her different poses' photographs are meticulously hanged on the wall among the chosen modern abstract paintings.)

Her house keeper enters with Kane. Audrey gets up and shakes hand with Kane. (Kane is meticulously dressed and looks very handsome.)

AUDREY

Welcome Mr. Kane. Anita talked to me that you are coming to my house for some legal issues to be sorted out. Our law firm is a leading one in the City. We would be pleased to render our best of services.

KANE

I am really pleased to meet you Ms. Audrey; you know that we who are from royal family have some feuds and internal rivalry for wealth and property. I am not an exception. (He heartily laughs.)

AUDREY

Mr. Kane we have to decide the priorities so that we could do a proper planning. I think you also need to appoint some sort of reliable detective firm to dig out information.

KANE

Correct. I have several problems and all are urgent. Let us look at them.

I am very eager to find out about my grandfather whose where about is a mystery after 9/11 attack. Our biggest business center is destroyed in Tower Two. It seems that all the staff inside perished; all the important papers, files and bank accounts and everything. My grandfather Mr. Kedarnath is the only person who knows about it as he was staying here and looked after the affairs. He spoke to me sometime back but I have not seen since long. That is a tragedy. We must find out whether he is alive and what happened to the important papers. Without this information we are in danger of losing our billions of dollars worth of business and property including the palace at Kedargadh.

He gets up and strolls, looks out and returns. Audrey is making notes.

AUDREY

We have to take help of Anita and her resources from Times. Times has extensive listings of everything regarding 9/11 attack. What is another issue? (She smokes. Kane is bit annoyed and moves his palm to disperse the spreading smoke from the cigarette.)

KANE

The second one is the matter of my life and death; it is to locate the family of my mother Nancy Jefferson. At any cost I want to find out her even from her grave. (He becomes emotional)

Audrey looks to him in surprise. Her professional attitude comes in her way. She has not seen man becoming emotional. Her disappointment is evident from her face and indifference.

AUDREY

Anything else we can do Mr. Kane for you?

(She gets up and throws her cigarette and lights another. A distinct disgust appears on his face.)

KANE

Very important to me what should we do for Anita? I am a stranger and you are her friend.

(He gets up and moves around her modeling postures in various photographs, stands there looking with interest.)

AUDREY

If I advise you then leave Anita to her fate. Cancer patient rarely survives.

(Kane is terribly shocked. He turns around from looking at photographs. He doesn't answer or wait; he just leaves. Audrey shrugs her shoulder.)

FADE OUT

FADE IN:

EXT: KANE'S CAR AT TIMES OFFICE, A DAY

Kane gets down and moves to the elevator.

CUT TO

INT: TIMES EDITORIAL OFFICE, A DAY

Camera covers her small cabin and it appears that there are papers strewn here and there.

Anita is shuffling papers; opens her drawer and takes out some more papers, clippings and other stuff. She is very seriously engrossed in her reading and examining papers.

Kane enters. Anita looks who has come in. She smiles.

ANITA

Oh. Kane it is a great surprise, anything pressing and urgent?

KANE

Yes. Can you join me right now, I propose to move around hospitals who have 9/11 patients under treatment.

ANITA

Kane (her voice is tender and caring) are you angry? What happened?

KANE

Nothing, are you coming or else I go?

Anita finds Kane is disturbed. She arranges her papers and put down them in a drawer; shut down her computer, quietly gets up and picks Kane's hand in her hand.

ANITA

Kane let us go.

Both leave the office.

FADE OUT

FADE IN:

EXT: THE CENTRAL PARK, A DAY

Kane and Anita stroll on the grass.

(Kane is serious and seems to be hurt. Anita observes him and her eyes are full of sympathy.)

ANITA

Kane, please tell me what has happened. I haven't seen you so serious. Has Audrey told you something?

KANE

Anita, I am hurt at Audrey's behavior. She was formal and indifferent. I went to her as your friend as you wanted me to seek her lawyer's firm involvement in sorting out my legal issues. Is it correct?

ANITA

Did she say something?

KANE

She didn't say anything; just ask me a few questions.

ANITA

That should not hurt you. Yours was the first meeting and she was formal that is natural. Were you sentimental about anything when you were talking?

KANE

Yes. I was. The issues are such that I opened up before her knowing that she is our friend.

Kane turns to Anita, looks at her. He moves closer to her and looks in her eyes. He keeps on looking.

ANITA

What are you looking at? Kane, my dear you can't be sentimental about anything. The world is funny and unconcerned.

KANE

But you and I are not; Anita, I can't be indifferent to anyone whom I know. I consider that all persons are basically good and friendly. Let us sit under that shade.

Both move and sit under the shade of a tree.

CUT TO

EXT: THE CENTRAL PARK, MOMENTS LATTER, A DAY

Ducks are swimming in the pond. They in group are moving to the side of feeders who feed them.

JUMP, CUT TO

EXT: THE CENTRAL PARK. WHERE KANE AND ANITA ARE SITTING

Anita takes Kane's hand in her palms and looks at him. Kane is lost in thoughts.

DISSOLVE TO

FLASHBACK

FADE IN:

EXT. THE POND, MORNING

Ducks are swimming and circling. A five year boy is heartily laughing and clapping. His mother comes. The boy runs to her and clings. The mother picks him up and kisses him. He kisses his mother. Ducks are swimming. Kane runs and picks up the boy and say, 'Hi'.

The boy is scarred and runs shouting 'Mom…. Mom'

He turns towards Anita and smiles.

KANE (TO ANITA)

See, he shouts 'Mom... Mom just as I shouted back years back to my mother.

DISSOLVE TO

FADE IN:

EXT: THE CENTRAL PARK. WHERE KANE AND ANITA ARE SITTING

Kane returns to Anita; place back his hand in her palms and hide his face in her two palms.

CAMERA ZOOMS IN ON THE CLOSE SHOT OF KANE AND FREEZE.

FADE IN:

Kane recovers, looks at Anita.

ANITA

I have a good suggestion. Why not three of us Audrey, you and me go for boating this evening?

Kane comes to his normal habit of laughing, says, 'Yes, why not? That is fine with me, if she is free and likes to join.

KANE

Well, the Prince is busy but I can make an exception to join the most beautiful women in New York.

He laughs.

FADE IN:

EXT: ON BOAT, LATE EVENING

THE SUN IS SETTING; THE BOAT PASSES CLOSE TO THE STATUE OF LIBERTY; THE TIDAL WAVES IN HUDSON AND BEAUTIFUL EVENING BREEZE SETS THE MOOD. ANDREW PLAYS GUITAR AND KANE IS LOST IN SEEING THE FADING BEAUTY OF THE GRATE CITY.

HE WHISTLES. TWO LADIES THEIR ARMS ON EACH OTHER GIVE BEAUTIFUL PROFILES AGAINST THE GOLDEN LIGHT OF THE SUNSET. THEY PASS UNDER THE BRIDGE; GRADUALLY THE SUN SETS AND THE BEAUTIFUL COLORS OF THE DUSK FIIL THE SKY.

THE CITY GETS NEW COLORS.

CAMERA MOVES ALMOST 360 DEGREES AND EVERY ONE IN THE BOAT SHOUT NEW YORK NEW YORK, SILENCE PREVAILS, ONLY ANDREW'S GUITAR AND HIS LOW VOICE SINGING JOINS THE BREEZE.

AUDREY

I have never experienced such a romantic moments in my life. How beautiful our City Looks!

(Audrey looks very beautiful and her hair flowing free in the breeze add to her charming face.)

Kane moves close to her; they face each other.

Kane looks straight into her eyes. She smiles; the evening faint colors close on both and Kane murmurs.

KANE

You are simply beautiful, very appealing, like poetry of my heart.

AUDREY

What a wonder! never thought that I would be with you.

CUT TO

INT: ON BOAT CABIN, NIGHT

CAMERA CLOSES ON ANITA, ALONE, SAD, TEARS ROLLING DOWN HER EYES, SOBBING.

CUT TO

EXT: ON BOAT DECK, NIGHT

FAR AWAY, THE CITY SPREADS SPLNDOR AND TALL BUILDINGS LOOK LOVELY; THE SKY LINE IS SIMPLY MARVELOUS. PLANES ARE LANDING OR DEPARTING.

CUT TO

INT: BOAT CABIN, DINNER TABLE, NIGHT

Dinner is ready; Anita is quiet and calm.

KANE

Anita, I am sure you must be finding lots of change. Look, you are fine and nothing is going to happen to you... We will have more such fun, OK.

ANITA

Kane, thanks for everything. It may be next time when only you and Audrey will be there.

(She weeps, wipes her tears. Kane and Audrey get up, go to her and console.)

FADE OUT

FADE IN:

EXT: ROAD: NIGHT

MERCEDES IS PASSING THROUGH MANHATTAN; STOPS; MOVES AND THEN HALTS.

EXT: NIGHT: OUTSIDE HOTEL HILTON

Kane gets down; talks to Andrew who is in the front and on the car wheel.

KANE

Andrew, please leave Anita at her place and see me tomorrow morning.

Waves to Anita inside, she smiles and waves back.

KANE (CONTD)

Good night. Take care of you.

MERCEDES MOVES ON.

CUT TO

INT: INSIDE KANE'S HOTEL HILTON MAIN ROOM, NIGHT

FROM THE LARGE FRENCH WINDOWS THE CITY'S PANORAMIC VIEW AT NIGHT IS GLORIOUS.

PROF. ROY IS SITTING AND SMOKING HIS PIPE. KANE TAKES HIS SEAT ON THE OPPOSITE SOFA CHAIR AND RELAXES.

KANE (CONT'D)

Prof. Roy, are you busy? If you have time I want to ask you. I have a dilemma.

PROF. ROY

Dilemma, what kind of dilemma, I have never heard such words from my dear Prince.

KANE

Prof. Roy I want to talk to you about Anita; that reporter, who is a cancer patient. She has a lung cancer and when I met oncologist Dr. Julie Roberts, she told me that Anita is in critical stage and her survival chances are rare.

He gets up, looks out through window and then proceeds further.

KANE (CONTD)

Prof. What worries me most is that Anita has only mother, her father died in war, her mother is also hospitalized and she doesn't have any idea that Anita is in critical stage.

He holds is head in anguish.

KANE (CONTD)

Doctor Julie told me that Anita needs a change; she has to be happy; you understand Prof that she may not survive.

PROF. ROY

What you propose to do, help her in what way?

(Professor is serious, puffs more and looks at the gorgeous painting of the palace at Kedarnath that is vast and expansive painting covering the wall.)

CAMERA CLOSE ON PROFESSOR'S BACK ZOOMS IN TO THE PAINTING.

HE IS LOOKING AT THE PALACE.

PROF. ROY (CONT'D)

Kane, think with the clear mind; do not be emotional. Please understand that you are in other nation and on definite missions. If you divert your mind and energy then what would be the result?

Have you thought of a disaster that may befall and ruin everything?

He turns to Kane.

PROF. ROY (CONTD)

May I ask you a personal question?

(Without waiting for Kane to respond)

PROF. ROY (CONTD)

Do you love that girl?

KANE

I do not. However, I am disturbed

PROF. ROY

Then, immediately withdraw yourself.

KANE

That is not possible, I may love her or may not but I cannot leave her alone in such conditions.

PROF. ROY

Humanity only does not work, Kane, it is difficult to decide but you have to think in a larger perspective, precisely about the looming large future.

You have to be serious about finding where about of Kedar; your mother and most important about your billionaire business empire; Kedargadh too.

KANE

You are telling me something that goes against your own morale and lifelong teaching.

PROF ROY

One has to weigh; what is desirable and what is not, End your dilemma.

KANE

Then what is your duty? You being human and stuck to be only selfish? Conveniently forget that somebody is going to die any time and you need to give her the best comforts and peace. Do you understand Prof?

(He shouts in anger.)

PROF. ROY

Then, if your heart and mind tell you what you should do, go ahead. I tell you to spend most of your time with her; take her on vacation. I will make the arrangement in our Manor on Hudson.

I understand your priority which is irrational but I love you and agree. Leave other things to me and go with her.

HE SMOKES DEEPLY AND THEN WALKS AWAY.

THE SCENE IS DISSOLVED WITH LOTS OF SMOKE CIRCLING ALL AROUND.

FADE OUT

FADE IN:

INT: KANE'CAR, ANITA INSIDE, ANDREW DRIVING, SAME TIME, NIGHT

(As Anita leaves Hilton hotel and is left alone, at back seat she slumps down and looks outside. She visualizes.)

ANITA

'What I am doing with Kane is correct? I know how long am I going to survive? Is not Audrey a right choice for Kane?

(She cannot control herself and weeps; Andrew looks back.

Andrew

I have never spoken to you but we know each other since our childhood; we were neighbors; I saw you several times and I liked looking at you, I had no guts or courage.

I simply request you to be calm and peaceful. God bless you.

(The Car Moves on)

Anita

Andrew, Thank you. I will control myself.

FADE OUT

FADE IN:

EXT: MONTGOMERY PLACE, NORTH HUDSON RIVER VALLEY

The scenic views, majestic old trees, and formal gardens of Montgomery Place make it an ideal, tranquil spot for enjoying nature and landscape.

Montgomery Place, a serene reflection of nearly 200 years of continuous family stewardship, is best known as a landscape influenced by the great Andrew Jackson Downing and an architectural landmark designed by Alexander Jackson Davis. But the totality of the estate - house, gardens, arboretum, woodlands, orchards, hamlet, and natural features - makes it a unique American treasure.

The 380-acre property is an amazingly intact example of Hudson Valley estate life. Each of the estate's features has a story to tell about changing American attitudes toward nature, landscape, and home design over time.

The mansion includes beautiful classical revival exteriors designed by Davis. Visible from the mansion's terrace and north pavilion are inspiring vistas of the Hudson River and Catskill Mountains.

The woodland trails, laid out more than 100 years ago, lead through a hemlock and mixed hardwood forest to the cascading waterfalls of the Saw Kill.

Lush perennial, annual, and herb gardens, designed in the early 20th century, give a delightful view into the colors, fragrances, and designs popular during America's estate garden era. Picturesque and productive orchards border the estate, and in season the delicious fruit is available at the Montgomery Place Orchards Farm Stand.

CAMERA COVERS

A PANORAMIC VIEW OF THE ESTATE

A LONG SHOT

FOUR HORSES' CARRIAGE IS DRIVEN; SLOWLY CAMERA ZOOMS IN; KANE, ANITA, ANDREW AND PROF. ROY ARE IN CARRAIGE; THEY ARE SEEN TALKING AMONG THEMSELV IN JOVIAL MOOD.

CARRIAGE ENTERS THE ESTATE GATE.

CUT TO

KANE PLAYING ON PIANO UNDER THE SHADE OF A TREE; ANITA IS LOST IN LISTENING, HER EYES ARE DREAMY.

ANITA

I will never leave this place.

I feel I am in heaven.

I want to be born again on such a lush estate.

Life, Love, Passions, Poetry and Music, you all come to me combine; give me your best. Make my life dreamy.

When the prince charming is besides me and he is lost in his music, nothing should disturb him.

(Kane listens, looks at her, dreamy eyes and smile.)

Anita slowly dances with the rhythm; she circles around Kumar and sings in a low voice.

Oh. My free bird,

Soar high.

Reach heaven.

Fulfill your dreams.

(She repeats)

Kane increases the tempo of the rhythm; his fingers try to catch Anita's words. Anita's movements become fast.

Anita breathing fast but sings:

Never to return,

Never to sing again,

Never to dance again,

Oh. Free bird soar high.

She falls down and breaths fast. Kane and Andrew rush; Kane lifts Anita in his hands and walks towards the manor.

CUT TO

EXT: THE SAME PLACE GARDEN, A DAY

A BENCH UNDER THE SHADE OF THE TREE; KANE AND ANDREW HELP ANITA TO RECLINE. HER EYES CLOSED.

KANE

Anita, dear, you should not be so careless.

Anita opens her eyes and sits.

ANITA

Kane, I have no words to thank you. Why have you brought me here? It is true that I overworked and doctor advised that I should have a vacation. However, Kane, I never dreamt that I would be in any Manor. You have fulfilled my life dream.

KANE

Anita, you badly needed the change. Thanks to Professor Roy, he suggested that we come here.

Anita, I am surprised why you thank me; I want to make you happy.

ANITA

Kane, when we first met at the central park, it was a great joke; you were funny, when you came down and looked in my eyes I felt that I know you from ages, we have met somewhere. You were not a stranger.

KANE

When I saw your pale face and deep eyes, inside, it stirred me, a slow tremor touched my heart throb.

ANITA

Was that sympathy?

KANE

No. Deep pain, inside.

ANITA

Why, you must have met many sick persons like me before?

KANE

I have not met many, however, meeting you and looking in your eyes I found loneliness, seeking someone you would like to be with you.

ANITA

Destiny!

Professor joins.

ANITA (CONT'D)

Professor I have not met you or heard about you.

PROF. ROY

Ma'am, I am a retired Professor of Literature and Philosophy from Tagore's University at Shantiniketan. I have been associated with this Royal Family since many years; even before the birth of Kane.

ANITA

Professor, how strange? Do you believe in destiny? Why different people have different destiny and turnings in their lives?

PROF. ROY (SMILES AND PUFFS AND CONTINUES.)

ROY

Anita, Destiny is the journey to our destination; turnings are the curves that one needs to take oneself to reach the goal; I mean goals of life. Your question is relevant. Why, different people have different destiny. (Laughs) Very simple, as different people have different faces and physics.

Anita you are fragile and delicate, if we walk in the garden, you will enjoy the morning sun and fragrance from flowers. The fragrance has the Divine message conveyed through the bloomed flower.

Come, I will support you; rest your hand on my shoulder and walk at your pace.

Anita gets up; Andrew and Roy support her and they start moving.

CUT TO

FADE IN: EXT: A DAY

A LUSH GARDEN, WITH TREES; BOUGHS; CREEPERS; FOLIAGE PROVIDES THE BACK DROP.

THERE IS A RIOT OF COLORS; BIRDS CHIRPING; BREEZE IS SLOW AND PLEASING; MILD SUNRAYS FILTER THROUGH THE BRANCHES OF THE TREE. (FALL IS YET TO BEGIN)

ROY and ANITA enter, slowly walking, Andrew following.

ANITA

Why God punishes a few selected people?

ROY

Punish? He rewards. Divine play is mysterious; every moment of our life pulsates with Divine love. His grace is a great solace.

ANITA

Reward, I do not agree.

(BREATHES FAST; ANNOYED)

Professor, you do not understand those who suffer.

ROY

There is no punishment, our Lord always rewards. He never knows how to punish.

ANITA

Professor, I ask you a direct question. Why Am I suffering? Why my treatment does not cure me?

Why Professor, why is it so? I pray to my Lord that I want to live, I want to love, I want to enjoy every moment of my life. (She sobs)

ROY

I ask you another personal question. Are you afraid of death?

(Anita screams wants to runs back; Andrew helps her; Roy puffs. Kane rush and supports Anita to walk hand in hand.)

Anita turns back and returns, wiping her tears.

ANITA

Yes, professor, I am afraid, I do not want to die so young.

ROY

My dear, life is uncertain, I suggest forget your diseases; more you remember your pain will grow, more it becomes acute. If you forget the pain and enjoy such beautiful and bountiful Nature, you will be relaxed. You have a company of Kane, his warmth and friendship; forget and enjoy.

I am little tough but it is true; I want you to believe in Him; remember all your silent prayers in the Church, every morning, every evening, every Sunday. Find peace within and live, death comes and goes away but the time does not, my dear sweet Anita.

(Anita moves close to Roy, place her hand on his shoulder, Roy blesses her and then embraces.)

ROY (CONTD)

Come my daughter, you know that I lost my daughter when she was in her teens. She was beautiful, her voice was melodious, one day she met with an accident before my eyes and passed away, I could not stop her passing away, forever.

I wept, and realize that everyone is alone in this journey of life.

ANITA

You have removed all my fears, father; you have given me new hopes.

CUT TO

FADE IN: EXT: DUSK

TARRY TOWN, SUNNY SIDE

HUDSON RIVER VALLEY

SIR WASHINGTON IRVING INN

THE LAMPS ARE LIGHTED AND FEW GROUPS OF TOURISTS ROAM; THE SOFT MUSIC FILLS THE AIR.

CUT TO

EXT THE OPEN GARDEN LATE EVENING

AUDREY ENTERS AND OCCUPIES ONE CHAIR AND LOOKS TO THE OPEN HORIZON IN THE WEST; GETS UP AND ROAMS. SHE IS WAITING FOR KANE AND OTHERS TO JOIN.

There enters the Mercedes and Kane waves to Audrey, She waves back. Andrew brings the Mercedes to halt and waits guests to get down, Kane gets down first, helps

Anita to get down, she is all smiles wearing a beautiful evening gown for the dinner; Roy follows and Andrew takes the car to the parking lot.

Anita runs and embraces Audrey, kiss her and catch her both hands and swings.

AUDREY

Welcome to everyone. I am happy, Anita is all cheers, Kane seems to have done a magic!

KANE

Not me, it is professor who has done a miracle.

ANITA

Oh, this evening is enchanting. However, it is evening. Let us forget everything and enjoy. This evening is memorable. Audrey, promise, our friendship remains ever so nice and committed.

AUDREY

I promise, we will love each other and understand and never forget our friendship.

KANE

Prof. Roy has a brilliant convincing power.

How about joining that orchestra? Let us move.

CUT TO

EXT; THE INN'S GARDEN NIGHT

BARDAVON HUDSON PHILHARMONIC IS ENTERTAINING SPECIAL ENTHUSIASTS WITH DIFFERENT MELODIES OF THE BY GONE YEAR.

(A Brief History of the Hudson Valley Philharmonic)

In 1932, four Poughkeepsie businessmen who were also dedicated string players--George Hagstrom, Sydney Fleishman, Charles T. Miller and Dr. Charles Hoffman formed the nucleus of local musicians that eventually evolved into the Duchess County Philharmonic Orchestra. With Hagstrom as its first conductor, the orchestra was made up of amateurs and professionals alike, plus a number of music students from surrounding high schools. In 1934, local backing enabled the DCPO to perform its first series of public concerts. By the 1940s, it had grown to 93 musicians. DCPO repertoire was largely classical, including some contemporary music and works by local composers.)

Kane and his party join. Roy is a scholar of Western classical music and enjoys; Audrey sitting next to Anita is attentive; Anita is more interested in Kane and sits very close to him. Kane is absorbed in melodious voice of the singer and is unaware of Anita. Anita tries to draw his attention by pointing something on the stage,

Kane listens but then he diverts back to music. Andrew standing behind enjoys music and taps with the rhythm.

One part of the program ends and the announcement says that another item will start after interval of fifteen minutes. Kane and party get up and go for a dinner table; Anita has her hand in Kane's hand; she wants to show that she is more close to Kane.

CUT TO

INT: IN SIDE IRVING'S LOUNGE NIGHT AFTER THE DINNER

AUDREY

Anita I am happy that you could find lot of change in last two days; Kane is very sympathetic; putting aside his own priorities, he has found time to be with us. That is great.

ANITA

He is great; he is highly considerate man and very humane.

AUDREY

Man or a person

(Both laugh heartily.)

ANITA

I want to share a secret

(Audrey remains silent with the expression that she already knows the secret.)

ANITA (CONTD)

I love Kane.

AUDREY

Does, he?

ANITA

I do not know that, however, my heart says so.

AUDREY

You are young and dream more; but life is different.

ANITA

Audrey, When some one comes to the wall and there is a total darkness, we try to get a small ray of light; a hope.

AUDREY

Not to be shattered; what I have learnt from my life is that one has to avoid the darkness; I mean our condition of life, our mind.

AUDREY (CONTD)

You know very well that you are a cancer patient in a critical condition; though our prayer is with you; you must face the situation.

I do not understand why you have imagined that Kane loves you. Kane is showing his exemplary humanity and nothing else.

ANITA

Unless someone loves you, nobody takes so much care of you; spends so many dollars; that he loves me it is beyond doubt. When we first met at the press conference at the Central Park, he looked in my eyes and there I saw a pure love; it is unfortunate that my ailment increased and I came to edges.

AUDREY

That might not have been love but pure sympathy; when he saw your pale face eyes, he helped you all along.

ANITA

Do not tell me that, you are wrong; I have seen many men in this City who show you that they love you but not. They want your friendship to enjoy, sex and everything.

AUDREY

That is his royal blood, his values of life, his innocence. He wants to make other people happy. He is not after mere physical pleasure. Do you understand?

ANITA

Sorry, I doubt, you love him too and that is why, that is why all this philosophizing, Audrey?

(She shouts and sobs)

Audrey gets up; putting her palms on her ears, not to listen; she is angry.

Andrew is in another chair behind them, removes the cover of newspaper and turns back.

FADE OUT:

FADE IN:

EXT: KANE'S HILTON SUIT MORNING

(Prof. Roy is busy reading newspapers; he is amused at one headline that reads with picture :)

'The Prince meets Ms. America.'

(Kane and Audrey are smiling to each other with Kane's hand on her shoulder.)

ROY

Kane, there is a tantalizing news for you.

He lights his pipe and smokes.

Kane enters wearing yellow silk Dhoti from pooja room, reciting Slokas.

He picks up the paper; he first laughs and then frowns.

KANE

These, media are going to drive me out of the City.

(He throws the paper. And continues)

KANE (CONTD)

That reminds me Professor that we have to meet Audrey's attorney firm to discuss the case of mom; Audrey told me that she would be willing to help us through her firm.

PROF ROY

I am happy that you have come back to yourself; away from that sick and mad girl.

We have a commitment, a mission to know that under what circumstances your mom died after giving you a birth.

No one knows in Kedargadh; and if someone who knew, that was Kedarnath, your grandfather, who rushed to New York and attended her funeral.

He brought to you to Kedargadh and handed over to Radhika; a trusted house keeper in the palace.

She looked after you. You always thought that Radhika is your mother.

The Palace intrigues were such that you need to be saved as an heir to the dynasty and on the other your father's affair with your mom should not been known to anyone. No one remembers your mom's name.

(Kane is serious and gloomy; gets up and goes away.)

CUT TO

INT: AUDREY'S CHAMBER AT HER OFFICE.DAY

Audrey lights a cigarette and goes through some important papers; as the file is marked confidential and important. With the file, she moves to and fro, her expression changes as she goes through the papers.

There enter Kane and Prof. Roy. She welcomes both and requests them to occupy their seats on a comfortable sofa set. Mr. Leslie, her partner enters and greets Kane and Roy.

LESLIE, a bulky man, smokes cheroot, has habit of laughing loud without any reason; he suddenly becomes serious and angry.

LESLIE

I must introduce our firm and we two who are the senior partners of this firm.

Audrey, incidentally whom you know as Ms. America is her recent laurel but she is one of the most respected and promising lawyer of New York. She is law graduate with distinction from Yale University. She is the daughter of Mr. Simpson Pricewater, who was a leading lawyer and a counsel to many wealthy people. I am proud to be associated with her as senior partner and assure you that we will try our best to get you the justice you want.

(AUDREY KEEPS ON SMILING.)

AUDREY

Kane and Prof Roy, Mr. Leslie has given formal introduction and it is my turn to say about Mr. Leslie. He is my uncle and a brother of my father. He is the outstanding lawyer in America specializing in investigative justice.

He is humorous and cordial person. I have learnt a lot about the profession under him in the last two years.

PROF. ROY

We are pleased to have met you this morning and are proud that we will be dealing with the renowned lawyer's firm.

It is customary that before we say about our legal issue, it would be in the fitness of the thing to introduce Kane and particularly the Prince, we are from a very modernized and sophisticated royal family of Kedargadh that was the State before India's independence came.

Kane is the only heir to royalty. He was born in New York and to an American mother called Nancy Jefferson. She died within a short time after giving birth to the Prince; unfortunately his father was not here and tragically died in air crash. This was 30 years before. His grandfather Kedarnath looked after Kane and gave him one of the best educations at Bombay University. He holds a Doctorate degree in Economics and Business. Besides he is a descendent of a royal dynasty, he is the heir to Kedargadh throne, the Palace and vast properties, there in India and at New York.

LESLIE

We are honored to have valued clients at our door that we will serve in highly professional way.

AUDREY

The legal issue, as I have understood from you, Kane, is to establish that you are the son of Nancy Jefferson; where are the relatives or cousins of Ms. Nancy? The records in the New York hospital where you were born; after all clarification sought, to establish your legal rights to your mother and your citizenship of USA; we need to find out any assets and liabilities your mother had and then at what stage these properties are and who manages them.

KANE

Audrey, I agree fully with your observation but to me what is important is to find out where was my mother?

Where was she staying; where could I see her face; where could I meet my relatives; to me the question of properties come late. Audrey, from the day I landed, I am searching my mother.

(Kane is bit emotional)

Audrey gets up and goes close to him.

AUDREY

I understand your inner feelings; now you are not alone and we are with you. Mr. Leslie has already commenced the search through our trusted persons; I am sure, soon we will have the information.

(The disturbed Kane looks in the eyes of Audrey; they look at each other.)

PROF. ROY

Where we meet; what we talk; what we find; or where we go should be confidential. This is the first condition

FADE OUT

FADE IN:

EXT. MERCEDES CAR; ANDREW DRIVING DAY

ANDREW

Sir, may I say something that I overheard at Washington Inn yesterday night?

KANE

Is that important?

ANDREW

I don't know what you discussed at Audrey' place but I am puzzled sir, will it be worth to tell you now?

KANE

Tell me.

ANDREW

Anita and Audrey were there, talking in raised voice; Anita said something that Audrey questioned.

KANE

Was that serious?

ANDREW

Yes Sir, Anita said she loves you and she believes that you love her; that hope is keeping her alive.

THE CAR CAME TO A HALT WITH SCREECH; JUST IN FRONT OF THE CAR AHEAD, SOME OLD LADY IS TRYING TO COMMIT SUICIDE BY PUSHING HERSELF UNDER THE CAR; SHE KNOCKED WITH THE CAR AND FELL UNCONSCIOUS. ANDREW AND OTHER DRIVERS HELPED THE LADY TO PULL HER OUT; SHE WAS BLEEDING; POLICE ARRIVED.

Kane came from the back and pushed Andrew.

KANE

Andrew, withdraw yourself, do not get involved, you have not knocked the woman. I want to return to the Hotel.

Andrew followed.

The large crowd collected.

CUT TO

FADE IN:

INT: INSIDE KANE'S CAR DAY

Kane is silent. Andrew wipes perspiration and is also serious, bit angry.

(Kane recollects what happened; for a moment, an old woman is seen falling under the car; other moment, Anita is seen; this is repeated. Kane is nervous.)

The car enters the Hotel's porch and stops.

FADE OUT:

FADE IN:

INT: NEW YORK PRESBYTERIAN HOSPITAL DR. JULIE ROBERTS CONSULTING ROOM DAY CLOUDY

Anita gives a bouquet of roses to Dr.Julie and smiles.

DR. JULIE

So, Anita you had a nice time.

ANITA

Yes, Doctor Julie; I never imagined that I would have such a fine treat by Kane; it has refreshed me; it has changed my total perspective.

DR JULIE

Anita. I am glad. I had presumed that a change and a pleasurable trip will definitely help you. I am proved right. (Laughs)

ANITA

Do not consider my question to be silly; but I need you ask that.

DR. JULIE

Go ahead; feel free.

ANITA

What are my chances to survive?

DR. JULIE

They are more hopeful than before.

ANITA

Doctor, I want to know the truth.

DR. JULIE (SMILING)

I do not know the Truth. May be no body's know the truth. Anita, if I am not bit rude, I have advised you before that you remove your negative thoughts.

You know very well that you are a lung's cancer patient; the test stopped responding giving the signal that you are in a critical situation.

You're overworked and stress has spoiled the chances. We advised you to take rest and relax; which you did not; we advised that you go for a vacation and you did; that has brought you a relief; and that is a good sign.

Anita you are only eighteen, you still have a strong will power and an emotional resistance to stop deteriorating condition; you have these two important aspects to save you from the disaster; so, you, and only you could help yourself.

Look, doctors are human beings, specialists; they pay their attention to bring improvement to the patients. Drugs and therapies are modern technological means to fight back the disease. However, it is human being that makes lots of change.

ANITA

I did not get the answer.

DOCTOR JULIE

Then, please find an answer.

Anita gets up takes back the bouquet of roses, turns back and leaves. FADE OUT

FADE IN:

EXT: ON ROAD CLOUDY DAY

AUDREY AND KANE ARE IN THE CAR; AUDREY IS DRIVING; A LONG SHOT SHOWS THAT THEY ARE ON THE WAY TO ALBANY, THEY CROSS THE ROAD SIGNS AND DRIVE.

THE SCENE DISSOLVES

FADE IN:

INT: KANE'S HOTEL HILTON SUIT CLOUDY DAY

Prof. Roy and Mr. Leslie are sipping the coffee.

Intermittently, Prof. Smokes the pipe and looks out of the window.

Mr. Leslie refers to the bunch of papers, picks up one pack of papers, read something, puts down, picks another, reads and puts down.

Mr. LESLIE

(His huge body makes him difficult change his position.)

The collected evidences clearly point out that Kane's mother stayed at Albany.

Ms. Nancy Jefferson was wealthy and possessed good number of properties.

One doubt persists and that her death as sudden as she gave birth to a child is not convincing. The hospital records show that she was found in a bathroom in fallen condition. She was brought out on the couch and doctors examined her and declared dead. The cause of the death shows that it was suffocation.

The police records show that the one witness, a sister looking after Ms. Nancy, recorded that she was all right, her blood pressure was normal; her pulse was normal. She talked normally to the sister; the sitter went out for a while and came back running, when heard that Nancy had been found dead in the bathroom. The police recorded the version of doctors who examined her was correct and that she died of suffocation.

Prof. Roy just listens and smokes; that irritates Mr. Leslie.

LESLIE

Prof. What I say does not convince you. You know how difficult it was to locate these old records.

Prof. Roy

Mr. Leslie your firm will be suitably paid for your extraordinary efforts. We are interested in evidence.

LESLIE

The evidence may be forth coming. (Lights his cheroot and smokes)

PROF. ROY

We will wait.

Mr. Leslie packs up all papers and says good-bye to Prof. He leaves, smoking heavily. That creates the circles of smoke.

Anita comes in; they cross each other; Mr. Leslie is surprised and raises his glass to see Anita very closely. Anita looks to the lawyer with suspicion. She avoids lots of smoke and coughs.

ANITA

Good morning Prof, I have just dropped in to tell everyone Hi. (She coughs loudly)

PROF. ROY

Anita, good, you have brought flowers for me. (Laughs)

I am so old and not so good looking, no body presents me with flowers. (Laughs again)

ANITA

Oh, no Prof. I am not offering these roses to you.

(The same Ross that she took back from Dr. Julie)

PROF. ROY

That you have brought for Kane.

Andrew enters and signs Professor to be quiet; Professor is puzzled, gets up and goes to Andrew. Anita turns to Andrew and is surprised as both Andrew and Professor are talking in the unspoken language.

(Andrew is trying to explain not to reveal where Kane is,)

ANITA

Is there any secret? Do you want to hide from me? Where is Kane?

She is annoyed; Andrew retires and Professor loiters, looking outside the windows.

PROF. ROY

No Anita, there cannot be any secret. Kane has gone for a stroll.

ANITA

Is this the time for a stroll? Never mind; tell him I had come to say hello to him; I should go; as I have to reach my office.

(She leaves.)

FADE OUT

FADE IN: ALBANY. ALBANY COUNTRY CLUB

VAN RENSSELAER BLVD DAY: SUNNY

WOLFERT'S ROOST COUNTRY CLUB

(Club History)

(The name "Wolferts Roost" was given to the estate formerly on these grounds by the late Governor of New York, David B. Hill when he acquired the property in 1892.

The unusually designed home reminded him of the home of a favorite literary character named Wolfert Acker from the works of Washington Irving. As the story goes, Wolfert Acker was a troubled Dutchman who was driven abroad by family feuds and wrangling neighbors. Wolfert retired to a mansion with a cockloft look and the bitter determination to live out the remainder of his days in peace and quiet — away from his nagging wife. In a token of that fixed purpose, he had inscribed over his door his favorite Dutch motto "Genoegen en Stil" — "Pleasure and Quiet". Today this motto is part of the Club's crest. The quiet enjoyment of friends sharing a common interest had its beginnings at Wolferts Roost on this day. Over the years, the Officers, Board of Governors, Membership, and Staff have committed themselves to maintaining this heritage and in the process have made our Country Club one of the finest in the Northeast.

As a social organization, Wolferts Roost had its origin in 1886 when the Albany Press Club was incorporated. The Club rooms were established on North Pearl Street in downtown Albany, later moving to Beaver Street and then State Street. In 1907, the club name was changed to The City Club of Albany. In 1914, the membership began to show an interest in the property of the late Governor David B. Hill. Called "Wolferts Roost" by the Governor, after the peaceful hideaway of a hapless character named Wolfert Acker, from the Washington Irving Tales, the estate enjoyed a majestic view of the Hudson and its beautiful valley below. On March 25, 1915, The City Club of Albany changed its name to Wolferts Roost, Inc. and shortly thereafter acquired the property so loved by the governor. The formal opening of Wolferts Roost Country Club, with its nine holes golf course, was held on September 11, 1915. Since those beginnings, the Club has grown and prospered, while remaining a peaceful hideaway so near, yet so far from the city below.)

Audrey and Kane arrive in their car and parks. They start walking.

They buy Flowers. They get into the car and drives.

They cross the Blvd. Turn to Menanda Road, off to Albany Rural Cemetery.

Kane is in blue jeans and white T-shirt, Audrey is in white dress.

They walk hand in hand and they are received by Laura Jefferson, younger sister of Nancy and Nancy's Younger brother Tom. Laura is around 60 years of age, slim, longish face, and blonde-haired woman, tall, talkative. Tom is around 50 years old, well built, bit bulky, quiet person.

(Quietness prevails. A mild breeze flows through cemetery.)

No one speaks; Laura leads them to Nancy Grave; Kane bends, on his knees and lights the candle; place wreath of flowers, Audrey sits beside him; lights another candle and place another wreath and both remain bowed down.

Tears flow from Laura's eyes and Tom hides his face.

CLOUDS GATHER, SUDDENLY IT DRIZZLES.

Audrey gets up and places her hand on Kane's shoulder and Kane slowly gets up, he is very serious; he places his hand around Audrey and they all start walking.

CAMERA CLOSES ON AUDREY AND KUMAR; THEIR FACES GET WET IN THE DRIZZLE THAT INCREASES. KANE STOPS; LOOKS BACK, MOVES BACK TO THE GRAVE AND TRY TO PROTECT THE EXTINGUISHING CANDLES.

CUT TO

FADE IN:

INT: LAURA'S HOUSE CLOUDY DAY AFTERNOON

(COUNTRY HOUSE WHERE NANCY STAYED)

CAMERA FOCUSES ON LARGE PORTRAIT OF NANCY

IT IS STILL FOR A FEW MOMENTS; FREEZE.

THEN MOVES BACK AND COVER THE LARGE FRAME THAT SHOWS THE ENTIRE

ROOM FROM THE ENTRANCE; A CANDLE IS
BURNING BELOW NANCY'S PORTRAIT.

LAURA

Audrey, we must thank you for taking lot of personal
trouble to locate us. We appreciate your all-gracious
gesture that brought back, the lost mother to a lost son.
(She breaks down.)

AUDREY (BIT EMOTIONALLY)

I must have done some good deeds in the past; what
wonders me is, from where Kane came; how we met,
how, today Kane could see her mother. He had no idea
of how she looks. It was during our long drive he opened
up and narrated his story.

For thirty years, the story was hidden from the world;
except Kane knew that he was born to an American
mother who died after giving him a birth. He did
not know until he went to college in Bombay that her
mother was American. He only knew that Radhika was
his mother.

Poor Radhika, a British nurse serving in the palace to
whom the charge of newborn Kane was given. Kane's
grandfather Kedar gave her a name Radhika and forever
there after Illya became Radhika. She nursed the baby
and she really became Kane's mother.

Kane has a long story of how he survived through all these years. No one knows that Kane's tender heart is bleeding inside from the many scars that have been inflicted on him. He was a victim of palace intrigues. The gentle Kane, always smiling, joking, never revealed what burns inside. (She sobs)

(Kane gets up, goes to her mother's portrait, in Indian tradition he folds his hand in pranam, an Indian gesture of showing respect. He stands there in silence.)

LAURA

Kane, this is all because God is great, he always helps worthy and our worship from heart, he is listening. We got this miracle, our son.

Kane, this is your house; all the property of your mother is listed in treasury and with attorney' firm. You are the heir to all her property.

KANE LISTENS BUT DO NOT REPLY; HE TURNS TO LAURA AND ACCORDING TO INDIAN TRADITION HE BOWS AND TOUCH HER FEET AS A MARK OF RESPECT TO SENIORS. HE GOES TO TOM AND DOES THE SAME. TOM EMBRACES HIM. LAURA KISSES HIM ON HIS CHEEKS.

KANE SWIFTLY TURNS BACK AND OUT TO HIS CAR; AUDREY IS ALREADY AT THE

WHEELS. KANE SITS CLOSE TO AUDREY ON THE FIRST SEATS; BOTH TIGHTENS THE BELTS AND WAVING TO LAURA AND TOM, THEY DRIVE AWAY.

CUT TO

FADE IN:

EXT: ON ROAD DAY: HEAVILY RAINING

(Difficult to drive)

Audrey parks the car at the roadside motel that is on cliff;

There is a tall tree on the cliff near the motel. They remain in their car for some time. It is raining with thunder.

IN CAR: OUTSIDE IT IS RAINING AND THUNDER.

AUDREY

We are caught.

KANE

Let us be together in this rare moments, Audrey.

(KANE LOOKS AT AUDREY; AUGREY DRAWS KANE CLOSE TO HER; SHE BENDS AND KISS HIM.)

AUDREY

I LOVE YOU.

KANE

I LOVE YOU TOO. AUDREY YOU ARE MINE: MY LIFE.

AUDREY

Lets us get out and drench ourselves forgetting everything.

KANE

Let us take shelter under that tree. I will play the Sitar; (The Indian String Instrument) this is the season to weep so that our heart becomes light and hearty.

Kane pulls out the Sitar; usually played by Pundit Ravi Shankar and other artists.

CUT TO

FADE IN:

EXT: RAINING, MORNING A SHADES UNDER THE TREE WITH RAINING ALL AROUND.

Kane is playing sitar, melodious Rag, Malhar: (A rag that is sung or played during Monsoon) Audrey sitting beside him. Suddenly Kane starts weeping; Audrey lays her head on his shoulder.

KANE

The music is my life; whenever I feel let down, I play sitar. I do not know whether these tears are the tears of joy of finding my mother or the tears of meeting you; whatever, Audrey, please promise that we will be together. My Indian upbringing has made me soft and tender; I love Nature, music and Indian Ragas that capture the moods of life.

For us everything is important; the dawn, the dusk, the evening, the night, the moon, the loneliness and the midnight when Lord Shiva dance with her consort Goddess Uma. Audrey, my traditions are rich and lead to inner contentment and Joy.

I am sorry, you may be finding me boring, extremely emotional and moody, but Audrey, the heart opens up only to Love that endures everything.

(He sobs while he speaks).

Audrey is quiet and has closed her eyes, her fingers moving in the drenched hair of Kane; the sitar is played, melodious tunes go on; the thunder and the rain stop; Kane put aside sitar and take Audrey into his arms and they kiss each other passionately.

CAMERA CLOSE AND FREEZE:

(In the background, the melodious tunes are becoming louder and then gradually fade away.)

DISSOLVE:

FADE IN:

EVENING:

INT: FIFTH AVENUE BERGDORF GOODMAN FASHION SHOW

AUDREY IS THE CHIEF GUEST AS MS. AMERICA

KANE, ANITA, PROF. ROY AND OTHERS ARE SEATED IN THE FIRST ROW. KANE IS INTRODUCED TO MANY CELEBRITIES BY

AUDREY AND ORGANIZERS. THE SHOW BEGINS.

AUDREY CLIMBS THE RAMP AND APPEARS IN DIFFERENT COSTUMES AND STYLES. THERE IS A LOUD APPLAUSE.

AUDREY LEAVES.

Then on ramp one after the other, models exhibit their latest collections.

Anita enjoys; keep her hand in Kane's hand. Kane is meticulously dressed; as the show is on and models come and go.

Lights on the stage change. (Kumar is bit disappointed. He shows that he does not like the half nude girls come and go; for a moment he feels illusion that these models have surrounded him and they are forcibly trying to make love to him, so many together.)

He screams

Audrey marks this; moves to Kane and they both walk away from the side.

Anita follows; Prof. Looks at them but remains seated.

CUT TO

EXT: HOTEL PORCH NIGHT:

AUDREY AND KANE WALK OUT OF THE HALL AND OUT ON THE ROAD; ANDREW BRINGS THE CAR AND DRIVES AWAY. ANITA IS LEFT IN THE PORCH.

CUT TO

INT: INSIDE THE CAR. NIGHT

AUDREY

What happened; why so suddenly you got disturbed?

KANE

Frankly, this fashion show does not appeal me. My values say that women are to be beautiful but never commercialize themselves.

I wanted to talk to you about Anita too.

She has declared that she loves me and I love her too; she tells everyone. Dr. Julie phoned me before we arrived at the show.

I hate her behavior. How long should I remain quiet? She is disillusioned completely.

(He looks out)

(Audrey puts her palm on Kane)

AUDREY (IN ANGER)

Forget. Do not give much importance to her. She has to realize that what she is doing amounts to black mailing you by finding an excuse of her deadly disease.

(She bangs her hand on the seat)

KANE

I do sympathize with her; I am doing what I can; but this is something that I cannot tolerate any more.

AUDREY

Suppose you tell her clearly that you do not love her; she is your friend and nothing more. You know at Irving Inn she quarreled with me. It has become impossible to talk to her or convince her.

KANE

Will she stand if I say that I do not love her? If something, happens to her? That idea scares me, Audrey.

AUDREY

Anita is following us in the cab.

Both look back from the rear screen; she is following.

AUDREY

We have to face her. Andrew drive fast; first be lost in the traffic; and if she is seen following, return to my apartment.

Andrew increases the speed.

KANE

I agree, Can we meet Dr. Julie and find out what can be done further. We cannot leave her alone in this condition. That would be unfair.

AUDREY

I talked to Doctor Julie when I found that the survival chances for Anita were minimal. She is in advanced stage and her lung cancer is non-small-cell type; it has spread. Chemotherapy, radiotherapy has stopped responding; only her will to fight back can give her little more time.

Kane I must warn you that please get away from emotions and guilt that you are doing nothing for Anita. Your help, understanding have helped her to survive, but how long? The end is clear.

KANE

Her hope, that, my love will help her to survive? If she dies and I tell her, I do not love her then. Will I be able to get away from the guilt that I became responsible for her end, though marginally?

AUDREY

DO I suggest? You may go back to India.

KANE

Audrey, how can I leave everything like this and run away?

ANITA'S CAB OVERTAKES THEIRS AND SHE WAVES THEM TO STOP. ANDREW TAKES HIS CAR ON SIDE AND STOPS. ANITA GETS DOWN, RUNS, AND EMBRACES KANE. SHE BREATHES HEAVILY AND THEN FALLS UNCONSCIOUS IN KANE'S HAND; KANE LIFTS HER UP, TAKES HER TO CAR AND THEY ALL DRIVE TO THE HOSPITAL

FADE OUT

FADE IN:

INT: HOSPITAL INTENSIVE CARE UNIT MIDNIGHT

THE LIGHTS ARE DIMMED; THE MONITOR IS ON ONE SIDE, SHOWS THE CHANGE IN HEART BEATS;

Dr. Julie and others doctors are discussing quietly in one corner, camera moves close to the patient; the patient has closed her eyes; Dr. Julie goes near to the window behind the patient bed and slowly opens the curtain.

In extreme dim light the moon light falls on the face of the patient; behind the panoramic cityscape is visible.

The patient opens her eyes and gives a smile to Dr, Julie, Dr. Julie moves close to the patient. Patient's eyes are searching somebody; Dr. Julie gives signal to the sister, she moves out.

There enters Kane, he is serious, he has a bouquet of flowers in his hand; as he enters, Dr. Julie is moving out. Kane moves close to Anita; she has under gone a final surgery and is very weak. Dr. Julie tells Kane that the operation has been done; they need to wait for few hours. She moves out.

Kane places the flowers on one side of Anita; she stretches her one hand and Kane takes that hand in his and press within his two palms.

Anita smiles she speaks slowly.

ANITA

No much time is left; we will be separated forever.

KANE

Till we breathe, we are alive and our life is a reality. Dear Anita, never in life to leave the hope; hope is eternal; faith in us and in Him are always combined.

ANITA

I beg you pardon, if I tell you what my heart wants to tell you in my last minutes.

Kane is quiet, moves forward, bends and kisses her on her chicks.

ANITA

I love you. Do you?

KANE

I do.

ANITA

When you say you love me; take me in your arms and kiss me a farewell.

Camera close: Kane slowly takes her in his arms and kiss her; the moon light covers the both. Kane then slowly places Anita on the bed and remains very close to her.

A smile appears on her lips. She closes her eyes and with a smile and wet lips quietly passes away. Kane, tears rolling down, covers Anita face and stand quietly.

IN SEQUENCE, THEIR PREVIOUS MEETINGS APPEAR AND DISAPPEAR.

(FLASHBACK)

DR. JULIE ENTERS, KANE DOES NOT RESPOND. DR. JULIE MOVES AND CLOSES THE CURTAIN. CAMERA FOCUS ON ALMOST DARK ROOM FOR FEW MOMENTS,

FADE OUT

FADE IN: EXT. HOSPITAL PARKING, MIDNIGHT

Kane gets into his car and drives away. Andrew wants him to stop; Audrey runs behind him but in vain, he drives away.

CUT TO

FADE IN:

EXT: ON ROAD MID NIGHT

Mercedes is seen driven at a high speed through Washington Bridge to Albany Off to Albany Rural Cemetery.

CAMERA MOVES AT CLOSE RANGE SHOWING KANE DRIVING

CHANGING STREET LIGHTS THAT PASS BY;

Camera some time zooms and show the various expressions on Kane's face; they are tense, anger, gesture of hands if asking questions to himself, on the way he throws out his tie, takes out coat and throws on rear seat, loosens buttons of the shirt, scramble through his hair and so on.

FADE OUT

FADE IN:

EXT: CEMETERY MOONLIGHT MIDNIGHT

Kane gets down from his car and starts to walk at slow pace towards Nancy's grave; he is totally shaken; exhausted and his eyes reddish and swollen. He quietly stands with folded hands before the grave for some time,

The voice of barking dogs are heard breaking the quietness of the place. On some graves still candles are burning flowers are strewn and fly over with the breeze. Kane sits on his knees and close his eyes and silently pray.

The shaken Kane standing before his mother's grave wait; he wanted to cry loudly but could not. He mustered the courage and sits on his knee before the grave and closes his eyes. In trembling low voice, he addresses his unseen mother.

KANE My mother, your son is before you.

How strange that I am before you at the midnight. I have never seen you, I have never met you. You are my mother. I am here to make a confession of a guilt I have committed just before a few hours. Mother I have promised a dying girl that I love him; Anita, mother she touched the depth of my heart. I was denying that I do not love her; but that was not true. I have never seen such complete and total love in any eyes. Our relationship was short lived. Anita took away my heart along with her. Audrey too loves me and I do love Audrey. Mother I love two women; Anita love was inseparable from me; Audrey love is just setting in. This is curious. I am confused. Mother I will never forget Anita and the last moments with her. I am terribly upset, mother no one is there to remove my confusion. I am completely broken. Do you hear me?

(He hears silent steps few yards away, a white light grows and scented smoke rises.)

He opens his eyes and he sees a tall white lady with a veil and a candle in her hand, slowly walking.

He stares at her. The lady in white moves closer to him then stops at some distance and speaks.

A LADY IN WHITE

My son I am your mother Nancy, my son I see your face for the first time. I have heard you; my son the Lord has given you an opportunity to be your true self.

Life is a miracle and a mystery. Life is transitory. Life has no relation. The birth is an accident.

My son, you have done a pious duty for a departing soul. Remember the final smile on her wet lips. How fortunate was she to part with the lover's parting kiss.

Love is greater then you or me.

My son no need for any repentance that sweet eighteen young beautiful woman has taught you what a true love is.

You came here to find me out and succeeded, for all these years I have been waiting for you. I wanted to reveal a secret that has become obscure.

Your father was not loyal to any woman or me. Your father was interested in my youth, my body and my property that ran into millions at that time. When I gave you birth, he was not there. Somebody tried to kill me in the bathroom. Luckily I escaped from the back side and ran for safety. Laura was there and she and Tom immediately rushed me to hide me. I survived and in disguise came to Albany. I was declared lost. You were brought to Albany by Laura as orphan and in secrecy we stayed for four years to gather.

That is my story.

She started walking back, slowly, with the candle in her hand.

Kane gets up and walks fast behind her. She stops, turns back and says.

NANCY

Wait, my son, my time is over, no need to follow me; I am only an illusion, a shadow; I do not have any body or a face. I was waiting for years to tell you the story. I have finished. I will never return; I will proceed on a new journey. Yes, I strongly advise you leave your guilt's and sentiments. You have to be a man, a Prince; you have to save your Kedargadh and save your mother Radhika, she is in trouble. Trust Audrey; love her, and do your duty. You are the heir to Royalty; your grandfather Kedarnath is waiting for you to help him. He too is in trouble. He is alive.

My blessings…. (The Words Echo and the cloud cover the Moon.)

The figure dissolves in the thin air and Kane returns.

CUT TO

EXT: CEMETERY, MIDNIGHT 2 O'CLOCK (THE SAME PLACE)

Audrey slowly moves to Kane; places her hand on his shoulders. Kane is frightened. Audrey smiles, takes him in embrace and kiss him passionately; Kane is trying to fizzle out from the grip; Audrey is amazed and in anger walks away to the waiting car.

Andrew is waiting at the gate of cemetery, holds Kane's hand, and takes him to the car. Audrey sitting silently beside Kane does not respond. He is tense, angry as his fist is tightly closed.

Camera closes on his fist.

(The sound of car being started is heard.)

FADEOUT/ **FADE IN:**

INT. KANE'S BED ROOM HILTON, NIGHT

Kane tries to sleep; the last moments of Anita come alive before his eyes; he opens his eyes. He gets up, moves to a table, opens a drawer and takes out Anita's photograph taken at Windsor INN in lighter moments. The close up of Anita with a lovely smile attracts; Kane takes the photograph with him to his bed, sits, press that photograph to his broad chest and then kisses the photograph passionately. He hears the light laughter of Anita in the room; he gets up; again hears the laughter and quickly moves to his pooja room; stands before the idol of Lord Krishna and weeps.

CUT TO

FADE IN:

INT: AUDREY MAIN SITTING ROOM ON THE PENTHOUSE MANHATTAN, MORNING

She looks at the far away horizon, suddenly withdraws and hides her face in anguish. She remembers Kane's behavior last night at Albany cemetery.

She is angry; walks back and forth; repeats, picks up the cell phone. There is a door bell, it rings and she moves to open the door. Prof. Roy is there.

AUDREY

Good morning Professor Roy; I just thought of talking to you.

ROY

Anything that is urgent?

AUDREY

Yes. I am very much confused with Kane's behavior; in fact, I am worried.

ROY

I came for that purpose too.

Roy sits on sofa and Audrey sits opposite to him.

ROY (CONT'D)

Before I say something about his behavior, I desire that I must take you into confidence.

AUDREY

Is it so, I do not know?

ROY

Yes. You Must know that Kane has never revealed the truth, why is he in New York.

AUDREY

Anything that is curious and legal?

ROY

Yes it is very serious.

AUDREY

Is it urgent too?

ROY

Audrey, Kane has been forcibly driven out from his palace and Kedargadh. His so called mother Radhika has skillfully taken advantage of simple and straightforward Kane who placed blind faith on her mother.

Kane mother has taken over the palace and all properties; they are in her name. The court issued the order. His grandfather Kedarnath where about are also not known.

Kane came to New York in this condition.

It was Anita, whose health became a matter of concern and we forgot everything.

AUDREY

However, that does not justify his rude behavior to me when I met him at midnight at cemetery where he had gone in most disturbed condition to his mother's grave leaving me and Andrew behind.

ROY

Is it so? I do not know anything.

AUDREY

He was shaken, broken and I wanted to give him solace and comfort, but he pushed me back and walked away.

(She sobs)

ROY

I know Kane; he will never behave in that manner especially with you, Audrey?

ROY GETS UP, LIGHTS HIS PIPE AND SMOKES. HE IS IN A PENSIVE MOOD.

CUT TO

FADE IN:

EXT: NEWYORK CEMETERY, EVENING

The church bell rings, the sun is setting down. The beautiful architecture is silhouetted in the sunset rays.

People are coming out of the prayer. Kane, Audrey, and Roy come out; they are serious.

ROY

Oh. Little girl, she is no more. God bless her.

AUDREY

This was not her age to die like this. She had many dreams, she wrote the daily notes; once I read, I found that she was far superior than her journalistic writing. That was a note, if I remember about her dream to be the princess and living fabulously in an enchanting palace.

(Kane is quiet, he is lost in his thought; both Audrey and Roy mark. All the three keep walking towards Anita's grave.)

Candles are lighted and bouquet has been placed, from long it is seen some body is sitting there on his knees.

All the three look at each other. Anita had no relative then who could be this man.

CUT TO

EXT: ANITA'S GRAVE, LATE EVENING

Kane, Audrey and Roy are walking toward the grave; they could see the back of the person. They reach there and bend on their knees in prayer.

A sob is heard; they open their eyes and they are surprised. Andrew is weeping, sitting with the folded hands. They go to him and Audrey consoles him. Roy comes forward and helps Andrew to get up.

ROY

Andrew, sorry she left us.

He looks at Andrew.

CAMERA CLOSE TO ANDREW

Andrew face is reddish and swollen; he has not slept for long time, his eyes are swollen too. He starts weeping loudly. Kane takes him in his embrace and they walk together.

CUT TO

FADE IN:

INT: CAR, LATE EVENING

KANE IS DRIVING. ANDREW IS BESIDE HIM.
AUDREY AND ROY ARE ON THE BACK SEAT.

Andrew opens up. His voice is gruff and he coughs as he speaks.

ANDREW

I beg your pardon Sir. I need not say to you. I am no body to say anything Sir. I had remained quiet and submissive Sir. I am a poor fallow and to say something to you is not fair.

KANE

Andrew it is better to share our grief and emotion. It is unimportant who is justified and who is not. All human beings are the same. We share feelings, emotions, thoughts and actions, as we are on this earth. There is no distinction in the eyes of our Lord. Please tell me why you are so emotional; I am disturbed at Anita's death, I am feeling a void in my life. It is very difficult to believe that she is no more.

(He wipes his eyes, while driving.)

ANDREW

Sir, I loved Anita. I loved her from our childhood.

Kane on hearing this breaks the speed of the car that gives jerks to everyone; he regains his composure and drives.

ANDREW (CONT'D)

Pardon me Sir, It is true that I loved her; she was my dream, my life, everything, Sir, I paid for her treatment, I paid for her education; only her mother knows. I never allowed Anita to know all this; I never wanted to be idle and worked very hard. I did several jobs to meet the expenses. She suggested approaching Ms. Judy to appoint me as your chauffeur. That is how I am here.

He turns and looks out.

IT IS DUSK; THE CITY IS COMING TO GLOW.

FADE OUT

FADE IN:

INT: AUDREY MAIN SITTING ROOM ON THE PENTHOUSE, MANHATTAN, NIGHT

KANE, AUDREY, ROY AND LESLIE ARE SITTING
IN THE CONFERENCE STYLE

LESLIE

Sir, it was very hard but we could locate the person
who knows about the papers that have list of properties
in America. They are secret papers and confidential.
Kedarnath only knows about these papers. These papers
have details about the palace and other properties
at Kedargadh. However, all these need to be verified.
A retired clerk n Chase Manhattan told me this
information as he was in need of money, which I paid.
However, that does not solve our problem immediately.

First, we have to find the old man, an attorney, who
knows the details and the name of the private bank
where these papers are supposed to be kept in the secret
locker with the code number.

ROY

This impossible task is to be made possible.

KANE

Leslie you and I are going by the morning flight to the
suspected destination. Professor you be here and try to
establish contacts with my grandfather Kedarnath. Try
to get the latest position from there. You may like to be
in touch with Rita, my friend and lawyer in India. I wish

that she should be given the entire task to meet mother Radhika and proceed further.

Audrey, you study all the papers and prepare a summary reports.

It is enough, we have to be on ground now and our mission has to be accomplice.

Roy claps.

ROY

Bravo.

AUDREY

Kane, in my opinion I should accompany you. We do not know what situation may arise, once we reach there. We have only few indications and we have to build our strategies instantly. My mind says Mr. Leslie could do many things but rapid action and legwork need two persons. I hope you do not mind.

ROY

Audrey is right.

KANE

I am concerned with work done, who ever may accompany anyone or me.

(Audrey did not like Kane's curt saying but she finally declared with emphatic tone.)

AUDREY

I am coming.

FADE OUT

FADE IN:

INT: KANE'S HILTON SITTING ROOM, MORNING

Ms. Judy is helping Kane to pack his luggage. The doorbell rings. Ms. Judy opens the door. The courier boy hands over the small packet to Judy. She hands over to Kane.

Kane is tying his necktie and looks at the packet. He just gets up. Judy is surprised and Kane unpacks the packet.

He takes out the wrapper and opens the box; he sits back and suddenly runs to his bedroom. Judy is simply amazed at Kane's behavior.

CUT TO

FADE IN:

INT: KANE'S BEDROOM, MORNING

Kane swiftly opens the drawer and takes out well-framed photograph of Anita. He sits on his bed and holding the photograph looks at the gift Anita has sent.

He places Anita's photograph on the bed, she is all smiles and winking her left eye.

He takes out a diamond ring in gold, and a golden cross; he starts reading a note that has come with the packet from Anita. He reads.

KANE

"My dear Kane

This is the surprise gift from me. I have bought it in haste, as time is short."

(Kane's eyes get wet)

(He reads further.)

'I wish I am alive to see you wearing this ring, I love diamond that for me is luxury but you are my Prince, you must wear the diamond ring in gold. This is for what you have done for me, a stranger."

(He sobs.)

(He reads further)

"This cross is there for you to wear all the time. This is my prayer for you and your wellbeing. Jesus' blessings will always be with you. My request is that though you are from different religion this universal symbol of Love will never come in your way, or values and beliefs.

Last, Kane, I will be always with you. Bye. Anita."

KANE WEPT LOUDLY.

ROY AND MS. JUDY RUSHED IN.

FADE OUT

FADE IN:

EXT: BUFFALO AIRPORT, MORNING

Kane, Audrey and Leslie arrive. They enter the lounge. Mr. Keith miller is waiting for them. He comes forward.

MR. KEITH

Welcome Mr. Kane and friends. I am Mr. Keith Miller. I have been deputed by your grandfather Kedarnath to help you in whatever the work you are here for.

KANE

Mr. Keith, it is nice to meet you. It surprises me. You mention my grandfather name and told me that he has deputed you to help me. Sorry, Mr. Keith unless I know your identity I cannot trust you.

(Mr. Keith takes out his identification card and smiles.)

KANE (CONT'D)

OK. I do not know where my grandfather is and how you come to know him.

KEITH

I do not know where he is but He phoned me and told that Professor Roy phoned him and that you are coming here and I have to help you.

KANE

Mr. Keith I hope you know the reason for our visit to Buffalo.

KEITH

Kedarnath told me that I have to arrange your meeting with Mr. Robins.

KANE

Who is Mr. Robins?

KEITH

Mr. Robins is your attorney who looked after your grandfather's business and properties here and some confidential matters pertaining to your royalty.

KANE

How do you know Mr. Robins?

KEITH

I served Mr. Robins as his personal secretary; he is now very old and had a stroke very recently.

KANE

That worries me, how is he now?

KEITH

I have not met him. I came to know from my friend.

KANE

Do you know where he stays?

KEITH

I do not know exactly but I know that he comes to Niagara Falls garden with his housekeeper most of the evenings.

Kane looks to Audrey and Leslie; they in turn look to him.

FADE OUT

FADE IN:

EXT: NIAGARA FALL, EVENING

Kane and Audrey walk to the fall and stand there. Leslie and Keith are discussing with gestures.

The beauty of Niagara fall and the sound fill the evening. The rain bow appears and arches Kane and Audrey.

CUT TO

EXT: GREEN LAWN NEAR THE FALL, EVENING

The green lawn has shadows of the trees and there enters an old man on wheel chair.

Camera zooms in to the old man.

Keith moves swiftly to the old man.

CUT TO

EXT: NIAGARA FALL, EVENING

KANE TURNS TO AUDREY AND THEY SMILE TO EACH OTHER

AUDREY

Kane I believe that our difficult work becomes easy. Look, when we arrive here, we were in dark; it was like taking the chance. What surprises me is when Roy knew where Mr. Kedarnath is; he never uttered about his whereabouts to us; not even to you.

KANE

Roy is a mysterious person. When we left India, my grandfather was not there. When we reached here, we got information that he has left to his friend's place. We did not know where he was. My grandfather is seventy years old and still strong. He has a habit of leaving Kedargadh without informing anyone except Roy.

AUDREY

Kane we have a terrible task before us. As you say that your mother has taken over the entire property at Kedargadh, she must have somebody assisting her. In presence of your grandfather, how dare she could take such step?

KANE

I never knew that she is a wicked woman, selfish, influenced by one Swami. That Swami is a notorious fellow. Radhika my mother who brought me up can do this? Wonder. He planned to kill me first. Radhika saved me. His next target was my grandfather; he fortunately escaped through his private counsel.

AUGREY

It seems that Keith has talked to that old man.

CUT TO

EXT: GREEN LAWN AT THE FALL, LATE EVENING

Kane, Audrey, Leslie join Keith who is with the old man.

All of them are shocked and look at each other; Mr. Robins is blank and try to speak but could not. His hands and face shake, his sight too is affected.

KEITH

I am sorry to say that Mr. Robins is sick and as I told him about your mission and urgency, he gestured that he does not know anything. His housekeeper told me that recently the stroke has affected his memory and he suffers from loss of memory.

(Audrey moves forward and places her hand on the shoulder of the old man; he feels relieved and gives a smile. Audrey sits beside him on the grass and pampers her hands and then kisses both of his hand. Mr. Robins with shaking hand bless her and tries to place his hand over her head as a show of affection.)

AUDREY

Uncle Robins, how are you, we feel sorry that you are having lots of pain. We are happy to see you and pray that God bless you, you find relief.

(Mr. Robins respond with the smile. He speaks to his housekeeper in broken words and looks to Audrey with affection.)

HOUSEKEEPER

Mr. Robins says that he is happy to meet you all. He is tired and if we could meet tomorrow morning at his place.

Mr. Robins tries to wave every one and his housekeeper pulls back his wheel chair.

FADE OUT

FADE IN:

INT: HOTEL AT NIAGARA FALL, AUDREY'S ROOM, NIGHT

Audrey is taking out clothes, wraps towel and opens the bath.

Audrey put on shower and takes bath.

Audrey is in bath tub; her body is transparent through water

CUT TO

INT: HOTEL AT NIAGARA FALL, KUMAR'S ROOM, NIGHT

Kane takes out his clothes with only underwear on the body,

He relaxes on sofa turns upside down and in reclining position opens the magazine.

Kane sits up.

The magazine shows photographs of nude and half nude women.

Kane enjoys and smiles.

(First time he likes nudity which he hated this hour, how the change came?)

Kane gets up. Stroll, he is amused. He likes to see those nude women. The idol of lord Krishna with Radha appears playing flute. A voice is heard, "man and woman are universal truth, they are there as Purush and Prakriti; the union between two is the secret of creation."

Kane is surprised and smiles. He thinks 'was he an orthodox idiot blindly following religion?". He realized that he repressed his true nature all the time. Why?

He wants to brush aside thoughts but they pursue.

'It is because he spent his life in uncertainty and was over powered by too much religiosity. His America visit worked to demolish many false notions which persisted for long time')

CUT TO

INT: AUDREY'ROOM, NIGHT

Kane quietly moves with underwear only to Audrey room opens the latch and enters.

Kane quietly switch off the lights except a small table lamp light. He sits quietly in one corner on sofa with legs on sofa folded.

Audrey opens the bath room door the bath room bluish lights fill the darkness. Audrey is not facing Kane and the dim light in room prevents clear vision.

Audrey in minimum clothes moves back in fear.

Audrey slowly moves to switch on the light on the wall.

Kane catches hold of Audrey's hand from the back.

Audrey loudly screams.

Kane puts his hand on her mouth and gradually lifts her up.

Audrey struggles to be free.

Kane takes Audrey near sofa and let loose her to fall on a sofa.

Audrey falls on sofa and springs back little in Kane's hand.

Audrey has nothing on her body.

Audrey sees Kane in underwear and wants to run.

She wriggles out and run.

Kane throws pillows on Audrey.

CUT TO

INT: AUDREY'S BED. NIGHT

Audrey jumps on the bed and shouts.

AUDREY

Kane, no

KANE

Yes, today, now.

AUDREY

What?

KANE

I need everything.

AUDREY

Kane is it you?

KANE

Yes, me the prince who only weeps for the women.

AUDREY

Come on Kane leave the joke what you propose to do?

KANE

What you propose to do?

AUDREY

Kane what has happened to you?

KANE

My Audrey you have broken my all-false notions and made me a man; I never knew what it means to love a woman.

AUDREY

Why so sudden change

KANE

You, Audrey you, awakened me from my slumber, my all false beliefs; my guilt feelings inculcated through my upbringing that sex is sin.

AUDREY

My Kane then let this night be yours and mine.

Kane then jumps into the bed.

FADE OUT

FADE IN:

INT: AUDREY'S BED ROOM, MORNING

Kane is lying on sofa still half asleep. Audrey nicely dressed and applying lipsticks on her lips; moves to Kane and plant a kiss on his both the cheeks and laughs.

Kane is awaken and yawns, still in his underwear. Audrey runs and brings mirror and shows Kane's face. Kane embraces Audrey and kiss her.

FADE OUT

FADE IN:

EXT: ROBINS HOUSE GARDEN, MORNING

Under the shade of the tree, Robins on his wheel chair awaits the arrival of Kane, Audrey and Leslie. They arrive in the car. Get down, walk to him and give him flowers.

ROBINS (BROKEN WORDS)

Kedarnath is my old friend. I call him Nath. (Breathes) I looked after his property and other legal issues. (Stops to recollect) I have not seen him from many months. Where is he? (Breathes)

KANE

We do not know. Robins, we are here to find out about our property and other details that are in vault in some bank. We understand that you have the knowledge of all the matters and detail. My grandfather is in trouble due to palace intrigues. I have come on a mission to find out. Your help and guidance are necessary.

LESLIE

From whatever information we have, the property list; the code number of the account are with some private bank. You may have the authentic information from you so we may get through the puzzle.

(Robins starts shaking and he is perspired. he wants to say something bur stutters.)

HOUSEKEEPER

We may have to stop here and allow him some rest. He is tired.

AUDREY MOVES FORWARD.

AUDREY

Are you OK Mr. Robins? Please be relaxed. You know we need your help. We do not desire to disturb you.

ROBINS

I am all right. The whole thing is highly confidential. It is dangerous too. If someone knows that I have given you the details, he will kill me. (He looks with fear)

CAMERA CLOSE ON ROBINS FACE HIS EXPRESSION OF FEAR AND TENSION ARE VISIBLE; HE PERSPIRE AND LOOKS LIKE A LUNATIC TO OTHERS.

KANE

Robins please do not worry. It will be highly confidential and you will be safe. If you want, I may arrange for your security.

ROBINS

I trust you I got the message from Roy this morning.

(He takes out an envelope and hand over to Kane

Keith takes Kane's signature on papers.

Audrey kisses the old man on his cheek and pampers his shaking hand.)

FADE OUT

FADE IN:

EXT: LONG ISLAND, NY, AFTERNOON

The Mercedes is moving fast. It stops near the bank. Kane, Audrey, Leslie get down. They enter the bank premises. No activity is seen that surprises them. They look at each other. They move further and are further surprised, the door is closed. They read the board

'THE BANK IS UNDER LIQUIDATION'

CONTACT THE LIQUIDATOR MR HAROLD

Leslie notes down the phone number. He takes out the cell phone and talk.

LESLIE

Am I speaking to Mr. Harold? I am Leslie, Partner, Audrey and Leslie Associates; we are a lawyer firm and we want an urgent appointment. Yes, I am speaking from the bank premises. OK. We will be there in another half an hour. Thank you.

FADE OUT

FADE IN:

EXT: THE WALL STREET, AFTERNOON

The Mercedes arrives. Andrew parks the car. Kane, Audrey and Leslie get down, starts moving.

FADE OUT

FADE IN:

INT: HAROLD OFFICE, AFTERNOON

Mr. Harold, (around forty), smart banker and investor receive them.

LESLIE

Hi, Mr. Harold, thanks for giving us an urgent appointment.

HAROLD

Welcome Mr. Kane, I am pleased to have your august presence here. I saw your photograph at Niagara Falls this morning in NEW YORK REPORTER.

Kane and Audrey looks to each other.

HAROLD

Mr. Kane, tell me what can I do for you.

KANE

Mr. Harold, coming straight to the business, we have our account with your bank and that is under liquidation. You are the Liquidator and we want to convey that we want to withdraw immediately our important documents from the safe vault. We have the details and other necessary information.

HAROLD

Mr. Kane that is not possible; unless, the court decides in the matter. That may take months.

LESLIE

If I may ask, what are the total liabilities that the bank has to dispose of and before what period?

HAROLD

Mr. Leslie, 757 million US dollars are payable to debtors with in fifteen days time. The closer of bank is almost two months old.

KANE

Someone is willing and wants to pay debtors their entire dues with damages, then?

HAROLD

The court may agree as the court is anxious to settle the issue.

KANE

We submit our application and affidavit before this evening that at our request the Honorable Court should give us hearing as early as possible and stop liquidation process before giving us the due hearing.

HAROLD

That is OK with me.

KANE

Thanks Mr. Harold. Mr. Leslie will do the needful as stipulated and discussed.

THEY COME OUT

FADE OUT

FADE IN:

EXT: THE WALL STREET, LATE AFTERNOON

Kane, Audrey and Leslie are about to enter the car suddenly there is a firing on them; Leslie hides him behind the lamp post Kane is the target; there is a second fire, Kane and Audrey run into nearby restaurant to take the shelter.

CUT TO

FADE IN:

INT: RESTAURANT, LATE AFTERNOON

The restaurant owner who has heard the firing outside recognizes Kane. He helps Kane and Audrey to go inside the kitchen. He follows behind them; whispers to them and come back on the counter.

The killers enter the restaurant with pistols and look for Kane and Andrew. They move around. Kane and Audrey have changed their dress, now they are serving clients in hotel dress.

The killers threaten the owner to surrender them and fires one round, in the mean time the police arrives and the killers escape.

FADE OUT

FADE IN:

INT: HOTEL HILTON KANE'S SITTING ROOM, EVENING

Leslie enters. Kane, Audrey and Roy are sitting, confused and tense.

LESLIE

I have submitted the papers to Mr. Harold and he will present them to the Court tomorrow.

AUDREY

Leslie uncle, how did you manage to escape?

LESLIE

I entered the back of Harold's office; he saw the firing and was worried; he helped me to prepare the papers.

KANE

We are being shadowed; we have to be extra careful. Audrey you will not move alone.

AUDREY

Kane we must inform police for their protection.

KANE

No. that will hinder and interfere our movement; we have to move fast. The killers wanted us to prevent any action on our part to lay our hands on our papers from that closed bank. It is definite that the information licked out.

KANE

I want to put our Manor on Hudson River for sale that should be place in tomorrow's newspapers. The sale is to close by tomorrow evening. That will bring at least three to four hundred million dollars.

I feel so pained that I had decided to donate that Manor in the memory of Anita for cancer patients and appointing Andrew as the manger and trustee. That is not possible immediately.

AUDREY

Kane I will add four or five hundred million dollars from my private trust. We must buy back that bank and salvage our precious papers on which you, your grandfather, your family and royalty so much depends. We will not allow our adversaries to succeed.

KANE

That is your madness; do not be emotional. I have no right-on your trust or your trust money.

AUDREY

Kane do not forget that you have every right on your Audrey.

KANE

Audrey we are friends, it will be haste on your part, if my grandfather knows that you gave your money he wail never pardon me.

AUDREY

I am sure that your grandfather will definitely admit me as your family members. (She smiles).

ROY

I have been listening to your valued dialogues and I am proud that both the characters perform well; now listen. Laura called me from Albany when you were not here. She informed me the 'Will' Nancy made and the investment thirty years ago has appreciated and that has grown to nine hundred millions. She has bequeathed that amount to Kane. She is transferring that amount to Kane's account immediately. That should solve your problem.

KANE

That is not fair. I will not allow that money to save Kedargadh property and palace. Kedargadh did grave injustice to my mother Nancy.

(He breaks down.)

He gets up and goes to his pooja room.

CUT TO

FADE IN:

He is standing with folded hands before the idol of Lord Krishna, tears rolling down.

KANE

Oh my lord, you gave us GITA; you taught us how to resolve the problem by leaving it to you. Your mercy and your grace is everywhere. The great love of my mother Nancy and her sermons to me on that moon light night have removed my all fears. I pray you to help me.

(He folds his hands again and stands there with closed eyes; he hears the sweet tune of Lord Krishna's flute; he opens his eyes.)

FADE OUT

FADE IN:

EXT: MANOR HUDSON RIVER, MORNING

Roy and Leslie are standing.

A beautiful manor in the background is visible.

A banner hangs 'manor for sale.)

Cars arrive.

People are visiting manor, they are discussing among themselves.

CUT TO

A Rolls-Royce arrives.

A tall handsome 70 years old man gets down.

Camera zooms on him and freeze.

He walks straight to Roy.

Roy introduces the old man to Leslie. Both shake hands.

CUT TO

The Mercedes arrive.

Kane and Audrey get down.

They walk to Roy and Leslie.

Kane is astonished and he moves and embraces Kedarnath, his grandfather. (He weeps like a child.)

Kedarnath

Kumar, my son I am here.

(Kedar has no knowledge that Kumar has changed his name to Kane)

KUMAR (KANE) Utters

"My prayer to Lord Krishna is working. I want to sell our property to save our property. We will get the highest price".

Another Rolls Royce arrives.

Everyone look at the guest.

Kedarnath moves forward and welcome him.

KEDAR

Kumar he is Mr. Ford, my friend and a billionaire businessperson from Florida. Mr. Ford, I bought this Manor fifty years before, when I started my firm K. K. International at New York as my personal residence. The time has come to sell it off. I remembered you as you are a fan of old manors. We have an urgency to sell this by today evening, if possible, to meet another commitment.

FORD

Nath, I am interested. I was your guest at the same Manor and we had many wonderful evenings. You arranged many evenings and invited best Indian singers and we all enjoyed. This Manor has nostalgic values. I am sorry that you have to part with your property. I offer eight hundred million dollars as a purchase price.

KEDAR

Roy, you announce this price and invite others if they want to offer more.

ROY AND LESLIE MAKE ANNONCEMENT

Other persons start leaving.

Roy receives a phone call on his cell phone. He talks.

A car arrives.

A swami gets down and offers nine hundred million dollars,

Kedar, Kumar, Roy and Ford are shocked.

Kedar comes forward.

KEDAR

I am sorry; I am withdrawing my offer to sell this Manor for personal reason. Any inconvenience caused to anybody may please forgive me. I have to take this decision at this moment as Roy tells me that this Manor is sold before anybody made up his mind to purchase.

Kedar walks to Ford and both leave in Ford's car.

Kumar, Audrey, Leslie are all perplexed at this sudden development

The swami in anger leaves.

Roy without wasting a single moment leaves with Leslie and follow the swami.

CUT TO

FADE IN:

EXT: ON ROAD TWO CARS, MORNING

ROY'S CAR CHASE SWAMI'S CAR

ROY PHONES KUMAR

ROY

Kumar, Roy here, now listen, immediately phone the police head quarter and inform to arrest the Swami. This is necessary. Tell them that you, the prince is speaking and your life is in danger.

CUT TO

EXT: ON ROAD, MORNING

FROM THE FAR, A ROLLS ROYCE IS COMING AT GREAT SPEED.

CUT TO

INT: INSIDE THE ROLLS ROYCE, MORNING

KEDAR

Ford, in any case we must contact the police and warn them against this Swami. He is a murderer of my son. He has helped my son's wife, Radhika, mother of Kumar to transfer the entire property at Kedargadh on her name. You understand why I withdrew the sell offer. This is urgent. Do you know anybody at the higher level who could take immediate action?

FORD

Yes.

(He phones and talks.)

FADE OUT

FADE IN:

INT: AUDREY'S PENT HOUSE, MORNING

KUMAR

(KANE) Audrey, now I understand who fired on us. That Swami is in New York. I am surprised how my grandfather suddenly came to Manor. Roy should not have taken such rash action. What shall we do?

AUDREY

In any case, we must stop liquidation of that bank. That is necessary. Kane I want you to be practical and pragmatic; we do not have time left.

KANE

What do you suggest?

AUDREY

Utilize the nine hundred dollars of your mother. If we save our property from the bank, we may be able to pay back every one.

KANE

That is my mother's money, American money; how do I spend that money to save my Indian property?

AUDREY

Kane, do you have any option; the presence of that Swami; the Court to be moved by tomorrow; stop liquidation; to save your life; to save your Grandfather's life. Kane, money is money, American or Indian.

KANE

Audrey, if one cannot stick to certain moral values in life, then what is the use of our education. I do believe that everyone has to face such situation in life, preservation of values are as important as our own life.

AUDREY

Too much philosophy in life creates nuisance value; make person inactive, force him to leave everything on destiny. I am sorry Kane; I will appreciate if you take the quick action. Your duty is to save your property, your palace, your family, yourself, your dear grandfather's life, help Radhika in time. I know that one has to perform one's duty, no matter, whether our action is right or wrong; what we do is justice or injustice.

KANE

What you are saying is the same what Lord Krishna tells Arjun in Gita.

AUDREY

That is the common sense, everyone's Gita. We here believe that we cannot be immoral to follow the cherished principles of life; we believe in timely action.

KANE

Who could have been a better adviser, guide, friend and philosopher then you, my dear Audrey?

FADE OUT

FADE IN:

INT: AUFREY OFFICE, MORNING

Audrey is busy looking into papers, gives instructions to staff. Leslie is having last minute discussion. Audrey's secretary checks that important papers are signed.

Audrey carefully place pay order of us dollars 760 millions in her executive bag,

She is dressed as a lawyer. She is tense and busy.

Harold enters. Shortly Audrey, Leslie and Harold leave.

FADE OUT

FADE IN:

EXT: CEMETARY, MORNING, BREEZY, CLOUDY

Kane walks slowly towards Anita grave, a tomb stone mentions;

'ANITA CHARLOTTE THE UNFINISHED POETRY OF LIFE'

(Kane is alone.)

KANE

(Kane lights a candle and place flowers.)

It is more than a week that we are not together.

I hope that you are experiencing the silence, the quietness that we never get when we are alive.

Anita, those last moments of your life when we kissed and embraced each other were the most pious moments. Yours and mine-wet lips are still not dried up; it will never be so.

My dear Anita I deeply feel that I loved you and only you.

Audrey came in my life and still we are together. She loves me and I too, however I have a very different feelings in my heart. It is not your death or any sympathy that you had cancer, Anita but a relationship suddenly woven among us that bound us forever.

I have come today because my two missions are over; one of finding out my lost mother and second to find out details of our property to restore the strength to my dying dynasty. I have done.

I found my Grand Father.

To leave you alone under this tomb under the eternal cold, silence, and go away pinches my heart. My heart bleeds.

I love New York and my stay at New York has bound me with this City forever. You and New York are inseparable to me.

Audrey loves me. She does not know that I told you the truth that I love you, that was our promise to each other that only you and I know.

Anita if I tell Audrey that I promised that I love you then how will she feels; her heart will be broken.

(Kane is all silence. He does not notice that Audrey listens to what he is saying. He turns and sees that Audrey is standing with flowers.)

AUDREY

Congratulations. Your job is done. Citizen's Island Bank is yours. Now is the time for you to take the formal charge and look for the papers you and your grandfather want.

She hands over the papers and smiles. She leaves, sits in the car and drives away.

FADE OUT

FADE IN:

INT: THE POLICE CUSTODY, MORNING

The swami is in lock up, moving back and forth in anger.

The police officer on duty is busy with the file; as he reads his expression changes, he looks at swami in disgust.

Kedar, Kumar, Roy enter and the police officer point to the swami, throws the file in anger on the table.

OFFICER

Sir, this Swami is criminal; there are several cases against him. I received a call from the Interpol that he is wanted in three-murder cases.

I must thank you that you alerted us and before he could emplane for India, we arrested him.

We have called you to verify that he is the same Swami.

He orders the parade and all the three identify him as the same swami. Kedar hands over the file containing photographs in various postures of the swami as more evidence. He requests the police officer.

KEDAR

If permissible as per the rule of USA and on international convention on such criminal, I request you sir that you should take initiative to alert the police authorities in India that his henchmen may be prevented from doing any harm to the lives and property at Kedargadh before I go back.

(They leave the police station. the swami bangs his chain in anger with the lock up gate.)

FADE OUT

FADE IN:

INT: THE SAME CEMETERY, THE CHURCH, MORNING

Kane enters, moves slowly, sits in prayer on the front bench. The morning light filters through stain glass window falls on Jesus.

KANE

OH Lord, forgive me. Save me from further sin. I pray for your mercy. You are the symbol of Love and this cross that is the parting gift from my Anita and this golden ring from her are binding us forever.

Give me courage to convince Audrey.

He gets up and begins to leave; a young priest comes, walks fast and place his hand on Kane's shoulder, Kane turns back, joins both the hands in Pranam and gives a smile.

THE PRIEST

My son courage, conviction and confidence are primary virtues for entire humanity. Trust yourself. Lead a life that gives fragrance to all whom you love and adore. I bless. Jesus and your Lord Krishna are the same. They manifest different religion but they are one. I know bit of your religion which teaches Universal Love and Brotherhood. It is said "AUM TAT SAT", "I am the Truth". One of your scripture says, "EKO HUM BAHU SYAM", "I AM ONE, MANIFESTED AS MANY". They are everywhere. Go home and do your duty.

He blesses Kane.

FADE OUT

FADE IN:

INT: KANE HILTON HOTEL SUITE, MAIN ROOM EVENING

Kedar is sitting on sofa below the giant painting of Kedargadh palace.

Roy is smoking pipe.

Kumar is silent sting on one sofa chair.

KEDAR

We have won on the entire front. When you and Roy reached America, I had lost all hope. I am returning to Kedargadh with all the papers as early as possible. I got the phone call from Rita that Radhika has been released but she is still unsafe.

Before I leave, I want you and Audrey to be engaged. I like her as a person. She is very intelligent, dedicated, and well mannered; I believe that you love her too. Roy told me that she is helping us through out and took extra pain to solve our problems. She was very keen to see that things go through without hurdle. With her stinted support, we won our case.

KUMAR

Grandfather Audrey is exceptional woman besides she is unparallel lawyer of distinction. Her strategies provided timely help. What Roy says is partly true.

Before you leave, I want to confess that I gave promise to a young dying cancer patient that I love her. Her name is Anita. On my promise, she passed away with a permanent last smile on her lips. She is quietly resting in her grave on that promise.

She loved me. She died at the age of just eighteen.

Her love has given me new insight; her love has made me a real man of action.

(He stops for some time and then proceeds)

Audrey too helped me to take action and leave inaction. These two women have taught me the great lessons of my life.

KEDAR

I understand my son; but we are from the great Royalty and we fought war, we won, we lost and we survived. We are Rajput blood, we never leave our battleground. We are always willing to lay our lives for our motherland.

KUMAR

I feel the Rajput blood flowing in my veins. I know I am the Prince, inheritor of our Royalty and Dynasty.

I am sorry to say that this Prince was neglected throughout; he was born to American woman whom no one cared to meet or keep relation with her. My father treated her as one of his extra marital object not even as human being! Attempt was made to kill her after her delivery so she may not claim anything in future on behalf of her son. She managed to escape and my aunt took me to her She was a daughter of a multi millionaire American businessperson and belonged to the respected family.

She took care of me till I was four. Then one day I was kidnapped and brought to Kedargadh. Her son was given opium so that he may remain deranged in his life. It was Radhika my mother and caretaker who save me. Do not forget that she too is not Rajput but a British Citizen. She served you and your palace and me on your request. She adopted your place and your family.

Tell me grandfather that what is important in life? That sweet parting smile of dying Anita, unreserved dedication of Audrey, though she is Ms. America, a beautiful model in the world and prominent lawyer or your Royalty and everything that goes with the Royalty where even the notorious Swami gets respect and power?

KEDAR

I am proud to hear my grandson; I am proud to hear him speak so frankly, without any fear or reservation. My son, the time has changed. No one talks of Royalty or Dynasty. It is all Democracy and people's power and privilege.

You know that I am aged and alone. There is no one to look after our huge palace and property. When I am not there what may happen to everything?

KUMAR

My grandfather, if I die like Anita, I ask you who will be there to look after the palace and property. More, they are becoming liabilities then assets or investment.

KEDAR

If you think so, you find your way and a lifestyle. However, may I ask you what you propose to do?

KUMAR

I want to be reasonably rich, earn through my ability as much as possible, enjoy the fruits of my own labor and serve the cause of humanity, particularly the prevention and care for Cancer patients.

My stay in America and in New York teaches me that I should leave where the society moves with the changing time. This is my New Testament.

ROY

Kedar, we both go back. Leave Kumar here; he will own the new bank and the Manor. He likes New York and he is a New Yorker in all sense.

The discussion suddenly stop, Audrey enters with flowers.

AUDREY

I have bought Flowers for Kedarnath, for Kane and for the Professor. Audrey and Leslie Associates are happy to serve you, the most respected client and for providing an experience that we will always treasure.

KANE is an exceptional man, who has his vision, values and conviction. He follows his heart more than his brain. However, that is his personal style. He is liberal, loyal and very good human being, rare to find these days.

He came to New York and adopted the City. He loves New York more than many of us who stays here for ages.

KUMAR (KANE)

So many compliments look business like. I do not know I deserve them.

KEDAR

Audrey, I heard the whole story. I will term it as a drama in one's life. I have seen many places, have met many people and have business deals with many world-renowned businesspersons.

What I did not see was the human side of the life. I was, unfortunately very far away from that. Kumar is lucky that he came here and saw the new world.

AUDREY

Mr. Kedarnath I also over heard your discussion, sitting in nearby room.

What I liked was the frank and cordial opinion of all. I have rarely seen such frank discussion in family. In America, we suffer from the family bond and family relations. Our thirst for Individualism has led our nation to commit many errors.

KEDAR

Our roles and relationships are complimentary. Both the nations have great future. In addition, what has happened in last few weeks have opened up new era.

Finally, I want to leave. I see that you and my son Kumar are complimentary to each other, like a symbol of days that are going to come. You have made the beginning. Keep it up.

I suggest Kumar to begin a new life with Audrey. You both love each other; you do not have fundamental differences and you are open. You know each other's personal life, there is no secret.

AUDREY

I fully endorse the new testament of Kane and bind myself to carry out what he believes and wants to do. In addition, finally, I deeply respect your love for Anita.

KUMAR (KANE)

Audrey, your help and your dedication to me are unique; I must confess that my love for Anita is becoming stronger every day. Under the circumstances, please consider that I may not justify our relationship as husband and wife.

AUDREY

I am also clear in my mind and heart that no other man can take your place in my life. If we do not marry then I will remain beside you as companion if you choose to be in America.

KUMAR (KANE)

NEW YORK is my city; my future will grow here. I want to serve the poor and sick; I will speed more time in social work that too will affect our relationship.

I will be where Anita is there.

AUDREY

I know that you love me, but Anita is your first love. I accept that relationship.

KEDAR

I tell you that you both are in love of each other. Kumar's fears are more illusory; his love for Anita will remain but Audrey will win over you.

KUMAR

Audrey, let us come closer; work together and let us be friend and companion.

KEDAR

That is the best solution. I prefer you both have to announce that you intend to be together. For society, that is necessary.

FADE OUT

FADE IN:

INT: HILTON HALL, EVENING

THE ENGAGEMENT CEREMONY IS ON; MANY GUEST COMPLIMENTS KUMAR AND AUDREY.

REPORTER

The Prince do you recollect our meetings at the Central Park?

KUMAR

Yes. Very well

REPORTER

How do you feel now?

KUMAR

I feel very happy. I want to convey that 'I LOVE NEW YORK'

I have coined a new phrase, "NEW YORK NEW YORK, WHERE THE HUDSON FLOWS".

REPORTER

Is this your message?

KUMAR

Yes.

New York and the Hudson go together, all along.

Audrey and Kumar exchange rings. Kumar has two rings on his fingers. Kumar kisses Audrey.

CUT TO

Andrew comes forward and blows trumpet. The hall is filled with music and laughter.

FADE OUT

FAFE IN

EXT: CEMETERY, LATE EVENING

AUDREY AND KUMAR OFFER FLOWERS TO ANITA'S TOMB: STAND THERE QUIETLY FOR SOME TIME.

FADE OUT

FADE IN:

The Church Bells ring; long shadows cover the grass; the darkness descend; the sun sets; the candle burns and shine Anita's tomb.

Printed in the United States
By Bookmasters